The Case of the Haunted Lighthouse

A Teen Gigi Mystery

Celinda Labrousse

Between the Presses

This book is dedicated to my Gigi Dorthy.

You are the inspiration and a light in this dark word. Thank you for being in my life.

Contents

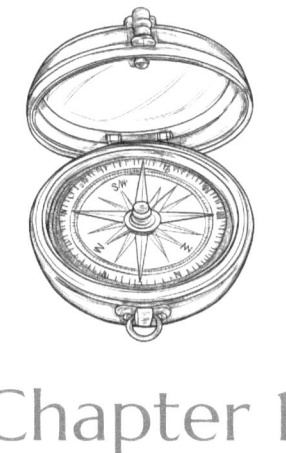

Chapter 1

The Missing Beacon

Gigi pulled her coat closer, the chill of the sea air sinking through her skin as she wandered the beach looking for her lost charge. The wool coat had once been the height of fashion when her father had ordered it for her mother, but it now showed unmistakable signs of age. Its deep forest green color had faded unevenly, with the cuffs and collar worn to a softened, almost threadbare state. Her father had ordered it from a Sears and Roebuck catalog with his first logging money. Logging had been good to them then. Now they were glad to have gotten through, and Gigi was glad to have a coat.

The mist hung heavy along the shore, casting Haven's Reach in a thick, white veil as the first waves of the incoming tide crept over the sand. Charlie hadn't shown up at school and was now late for their clamming expedition, which was beyond weird, since clamming was his favorite activity. They'd been planning it for months. It had been all the eight-year-old had talked about, outside his obsession with rocks and the caves he found them in. With each step, Gigi let her boots sink into the wet sand, breathing in the ocean's salty tang and letting the waves' rhythm calm her restless mind.

The beach had always been their place—first hers and Willie's, now hers and Charlie's. On late winter mornings just like this, Gigi remembered racing along the shore, shouting over the roar of the surf with Willi. They would scour the sand for treasures brought in by the tide. Once at home, Willi would weave stories about the bits of driftwood and seashells they found that day, dreaming up mysteries to solve. Pirates were a favorite of Willie's. She could almost hear his voice, strong and carefree, calling her name as he waved her over to the latest discovery in their never-ending adventure—a tradition she'd carried on with Charlie in Willie's honor.

But this morning felt different. The beach was still, too still, as if holding its breath. The fog pressed in, shrouding the world in a quiet that was more eerie than peaceful. A lone seabird cried somewhere in the distance, its voice mournful as it cut through the silence, and Gigi shivered. She'd walked this path countless times, but today, every step felt like a plunge into the unknown, as if the beach had secrets it wasn't ready to share.

As she rounded a bend near the rocky outcrop, voices drifted toward her from somewhere in the mist. She froze, listening intently. Two men, their voices low and urgent, were deep in conversation just beyond the line of rocks.

"It's the hull of The Golden Anchor, washed up out of nowhere," one of the men said, his voice rough with disbelief. "Thought that thing was lost for good."

Gigi's heart jolted. The Golden Anchor was her brother's old ship. He'd been barely 14 when he'd signed on his first voyage. First and last it would turn out, but that was another story. Gigi stumbled forward, willing the nonexistent breeze to carry more of their conversation to her.

"A hull that be only pieces. Barely enough to call it a wreck. Poor girl." Her breath caught as the words sank in, a cold thrill running down her spine. That ship was the last place Willie had been seen, disappearing into the fog and waves nearly two years ago. The townsfolk had accepted it as a tragic accident, but Gigi never could. She'd held on to hope, clung to every possibility, however slim, that Willie might somehow be alive. And now, against all odds, the wreck of his ship had returned.

She stepped closer, her boots crunching softly in the sand, just enough to catch a few more snippets of their conversation.

"Strangest thing," the second voice said, a note of unease lacing his words. "No sign of a storm or high tide that could've dragged it in. Just showed up... like it wanted to be found."

The first man scoffed, though his tone betrayed his nerves. "Maybe it's bad luck to be talking about it. You know what they say—don't go walking on old bones lest you wake ghosts."

A shiver ran through Gigi's bones, but she pushed the fear aside, focusing on her chest's sharp edge of excitement. This was no coincidence. It couldn't be. She turned away before they could notice her, setting off down the beach at a quicker pace, her mind spinning with questions. If the hull of The Golden Anchor had reappeared, there had to be a reason. And if there was even the slightest chance that it held clues about Willie, she wouldn't miss it. Charlie was probably sick at home today. Gigi made a mental note to check in on him later. At that moment, she had a much more pressing matter.

The fog grew thicker as she approached the far end of the beach, shrouding the massive, broken form of the ship's hull in a ghostly haze. It lay half-buried in the sand, its wood weathered and splintered, the remains of The Golden Anchor transformed into something majestic and haunting. Gigi stopped a few feet away, her gaze sweeping over the wreck, her heart pounding as she searched for any sign, any trace that might point her to Willie.

Steeling herself, Gigi stepped closer, her eyes catching on strange, almost deliberate markings along the side of the hull. She squinted, tracing the symbols with her gaze. They were faint, barely visible in the fog, and worn by the salt air, but she recognized them. They looked eerily similar to the symbols she and Willie had found on a piece of driftwood all those winters ago, the ones he'd convinced her were part of some grand pirate mystery.

A small, fragile hope flickered to life in her chest. Maybe these symbols were the message she'd been waiting for—a sign from Willie. She reached out, her fingers brushing against the rough wood as if by touching it, she could bridge the distance between them.

Just then, a shadow moved at the edge of her vision. She turned, her heart racing, but the mist revealed nothing more than empty sand and swirling fog. She scanned the beach, her instincts pricking with unease. Had she imagined it? The beach stretched empty before her, yet the feeling of being watched lingered.

Gigi took a shaky breath, willing her pulse to steady. She couldn't let nerves get the better of her, not now. She turned back to the hull, her hand trailing over the symbols, committing them to memory. The tide was coming in. She needed to get back to shore before this beach became a waterway again. She took one last look at the ship. She wondered if it would still be there tomorrow for Louisa and her to explore or if it would vanish again, taking her brother's memory back with it.

"Look what we have here," one of the voices from earlier broke through the fog's quiet. An arm reached for her, the mist obscuring the owner. She tripped back, falling down into the sand. She struggled, thrashing against the rising tide. Every wave turned the ground into quicksand.

"It's a fish on a hook."

"More like a guppy." Both men laughed as Gigi managed to break free momentarily, stumbling forward into the mist.

Another shadow appeared in front of her, blocking her path. She spun, sand slipping under her feet, her heart racing as two more figures closed in from behind their laughter, adding to the rising din.

"I wouldn't do that, love," a new voice said. Gigi's mind raced. She could run into the surf or head toward the cliffs—but she knew the cliff paths were slick and treacherous this late in the day. Her gaze darted toward the surf, and her instincts took over. The cliff was her only option in this fog. There was a cave she used to play pirates in with Willie. The one time they'd been trapped out here too long, it had been their refuge. Maybe it could be that for her again today.

"Crazy girl," one of her pursuers shouted. She heard cursing behind her, followed by splashing footsteps. She stumbled forward, scrambling for anything to keep her feet from sinking further in the muck. Water surged around her as she struggled to keep her head in the rising tide. Her heart raced as she waddled more than ran from the figures closing in behind her. The sound of their footsteps squishing through the muck faded, and Gigi risked a glance back. Shadows moved in the mist, scanning the shoreline, but they hadn't yet spotted her in the fog. Gulping air, she trudged on, using all her strength to pull herself farther along the rocky coast until she could see the mouth of the hidden cave.

Her lungs burned as she pulled herself over the jagged rocks at the cave's entrance, half-crawling, half-stumbling into the narrow shelter of the stone walls. The tide was even higher now. If she were lucky the men would have given up rather than gotten this wet. Gigi pressed herself against the rough rock, listening intently. The distant shouts grew fainter; her pursuers had lost her trail. She took a shuddering breath. How would she get out of here? Wet as she was, this late in winter, was a death sentence. It had been morning tide and mid-summer when she'd been stuck here with Willie. Gigi shivered from the cold. If she didn't get warm soon, she might freeze to death. But the water was way past walkable now. A passing boat would be her only hope.

Movement near the cave entrance caught her eye. Before she could fully process what she saw, a loud crack split the silence, echoing through the cave. Gigi flattened against the rock, clutching the wall as a shadow loomed near the entrance.

Gigi held her breath, pressing into the rock's jagged crevices as the shadow moved closer. Her heartbeat thundered in her ears, drowning out the distant crash of waves. The figure paused at the cave's entrance, head turning as if scanning the shadows. Gigi forced herself to stay still, though her fingers itched to grab a sharp stone. She tried to grip something on the floor around her, a rock, anything. Her fingers came away with nothing. She willed herself to remain calm. She was not going to die today. Not when she'd gotten her first clue as to her missing brother.

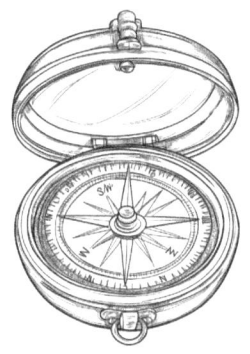

Chapter 2

Whispers in the Waves

The fog shifted, revealing a man in a boat. Half-veiled, his form was barely distinguishable against the gray haze of the harbor. In the mist, the boat's once-vibrant coral paint appeared dulled and ghostly, and the man was a silhouette like something out of a moving picture.

"Ahoy there!" Gigi bit down and gasped; it was a voice she recognized. Relief flooded her. She'd been rescued. As she moved away, a glint of something metallic caught her eye near the rocks where the figure had been standing. She crouched down, brushing the sand aside to reveal a rusted compass, its lid cracked, the glass fogged with age. She picked it up, turning it over in her hands. It was old and worn and looked like it had been lost to the sea for years. But it felt too convenient, too perfectly placed. Another coincidence? Or something else?

Tucking the compass into her pocket, Gigi rose and stepped out onto the waiting boat. Now that the tide had come in, the slough was flooded enough for a small boat to travel.

"Well, you look like a drowned rat," Mr. Thornton said, offering her a hand. She took it. The craft rocked back and forth under her added weight. She wasn't light for all she was barely five feet on her tiptoes. "Get trapped by the tide, did you?" Gigi nodded.

The little fishing boat drifted forward. She braced herself against one of the wood planks that served as a bench. Gigi could see patches where the hull was worn down to bare wood, weathered by years of salt and brine. She could smell the faintly peculiar odor—a mix of fish, seaweed, and something else—musky and unsettling, clinging to the air around the boat. She couldn't quite place it, but it was sharp enough to linger even in the damp fog.

Mr. Thornton sat alone in the boat; his silhouette hunched as he tied off a line with methodical precision—a crab pot by the look of the netting. Two buckets of clams sat between them. He must have had the same idea she'd had. A cap was pulled low over his eyes, but Gigi could see the hard lines of his face, softened only slightly by the rising tide that rocked the boat in a steady rhythm. The mist clung to his shoulders like a shroud, blending him into the hazy morning.

Gigi leaned a little closer, squinting at the knot Mr. Thornton was tying.

"That's an unusual knot," she remarked. Gigi knew a lot about knots. Growing up, her father had taught her the basics—how to secure a line, tie a quick-release knot in a pinch, and even the intricate sailor's hitch for handling rough waters. As a logging man, he knew a lot about handy things. He'd taught them to Willie, but when Willie was gone, he turned his attention to her. But there was only so much a logger knew about ropes. Over the years, she'd picked up an array of knots from sailors, fishermen, and even a suspiciously cagey dockhand who once showed her how to tie a knot that could be untied with a single tug, "just in case," he'd whispered with a wink.

She fidgeted with the foot of rope she always kept in her pocket. Her hands ached to try this new knot. If only there were a book on knots at the library. Willie used to drag her there before, but now she dragged Charlie. She might not have been the best at reading, but she knew when a little boy needed more schooling. Maybe they'd both have had a better time if more books about knots existed. Knots fascinated her; each one was like a little puzzle, with its purpose and history. She knew that knots, like people, had quirks and secrets. And sometimes, they unraveled in unexpected ways.

Mr. Thornton glanced up, his eyes sharp and appraising. "This here's a rolling hitch," he said, pulling the rope taut. "Good for keeping things from slipping—especially in weather like this." He nodded toward the choppy, mist-covered water, a smirk just hinting at the corner of his mouth. "You wouldn't believe how many people get caught with their lines undone. A proper knot can mean the difference between keeping your catch or watching it drift off."

She tilted her head, intrigued. "Do you have a favorite knot?

Mr. Thornton let out a low chuckle. "I s'pose," he admitted, tying off another line with deft fingers. "I am partial to the bowline. They call it the 'king of knots' for a reason—strong, easy to untie, even after it's been under strain." Gigi's curiosity piqued.

"Plenty of stories behind knots," he nodded, giving the rope a firm tug. "They say this here is the knot the old sailors used. Back when pirates roamed these waters."

Gigi nodded, her eyebrows raised to show her curiosity. Finished tying up his catch, Mr. Thornton picked up a pair of well-worn oars and started moving them up the slough, a glint in his eye.

"Oh, aye. Just ask any of the old-timers. They'll tell you tales of treasure buried along these shores, hidden by the likes of Captain Crooktail and his crew. They say Crooktail favored these waters, leaving a chest or two tucked away in the caves up the coast." The oars sliced through the water with steady purpose, each dip and pull revealing the wear of countless journeys. Their once-polished wood was now bleached and rough, mottled with patches where the varnish had long since worn away, leaving the grain exposed to the elements. The handles had grooves shaped by calloused hands over the years, fitting snugly into their rower's grip like old friends.

Gigi leaned in, wrapped up in his words. She wondered if anyone had found anything.

"You might be thinking, if the story's true, shouldn't someone have found something by now?" he replied, his voice low. He leaned in close with the next stroke of his oars. "Not that I've heard. Being the local historian and all, I'd be the first one they'd ask about it. But they say if you wander too close to some of those caves, especially at night, you'll hear the creak of an old ship's hull or catch the smell of gunpowder, even after all these years."

She shivered, glancing over her shoulder toward the rocky shoreline barely visible through the fog. Silence stretched between them, cut only by the regular splash of the oars into the water. With each powerful stroke, the oars creaked softly, the water catching on minor nicks and divots along the blades—reminders of rocks, docks, and the tests of time. The oars moved with a tired grace, weathered but reliable, pushing the boat forward through calm and choppy waters alike.

"What about wrecks?" Mr. Thornton turned to Gigi as she broke the silence.

"Did you see any?" she dared to ask.

"Oh, sure. Shipwrecks bring ghosts," Mr. Thornton said, his voice dropping to a low murmur as though sharing a secret. "We have plenty of stories like that up and down the coast. Why, the native tribes are best known for their ghost tales! Did you know that they believe spirits guard the burial sites of their dead?" He leaned forward, the fog swirling around him, casting shadows over his face. "They say the spirits watch over not just the graves, but all who dare to set foot on their sacred land. Strange lights, whispers in the wind, shadows that don't belong to any living soul. They protect what's been buried, both from treasure hunters and, well... curious souls like you."

Gigi shivered despite herself, glancing around the misty harbor. "So you're telling me this land is teeming with stories?"

"Aye, stories enough to fill a book," he replied with a smirk, his eyes gleaming. "But none quite as good as a pirate's. Those old captains and their crews—superstitious, every last one of them. They believed that anyone who dared disturb their hoards would be cursed. Some even thought the souls of their own men, the ones they'd betrayed or left behind, would rise to protect their buried loot." Gigi nodded. Her brother used to tell her the same tales. Part of her wished the old historian had something new to add. Something she hadn't heard before.

"What were you doing out here, anyway?" Mr. Thornton asked, his voice thick with suspicion as he glanced at her.

"Clamming," Gigi replied simply. His eyes flicked down to her hands, still remarkably clean for someone claiming to have been digging through wet sand and muck. Her outfit matched the bill, though. She'd be over the washboard to get the stains out.

"No luck?" he asked, raising an eyebrow.

She nodded, a touch embarrassed. Clamming was supposed to be easy—especially if you had a partner—but the beach had been empty when she arrived. Charlie had been so excited, and then not shown up. The only reasons Gigi could come up with were either he got sick or got sick of waiting for her. She'd gone looking for him but found the shipwreck instead.

Mr. Thornton gave her a once-over, the look assessing, even if his face was impassive, and then turned his attention back to rowing. Silence stretched out between them, broken only by the splash of the oars and the faint creak of the boat.

"A girl like you shouldn't be doing stuff like that alone. You need a partner," he muttered after a while. When she didn't respond, he shot her another sidelong glance. "What happened? Your friend leave you high and dry? Not much of a friend, then."

"Charge," she corrected, lips pressing into a thin line. "He didn't show." She paused, considering her next words. "You didn't happen to save any other unfortunate souls today, did you? A boy about aye high?" She lifted her arm to mark how tall Charlie was. Which, like her, wasn't all that tall for his years.

Mr. Thornton let out a low chuckle, his gaze fixed ahead as he kept the rhythm steady. "Only you, as far as I know," he replied. "But plenty get stranded or turned around out here. This fog, the tides—they don't exactly make things easy. People think it's a friendly shore till it decides it isn't. Let's pray that he didn't come out."

He eyed her again, his expression unreadable. "You're lucky you ran into me. Some folks don't have such good fortune around these parts. And some," he added, his voice dropping a notch, "don't run into anyone at all."

As the boat neared the dock, Mr. Thornton's face grew more serious, the lines around his eyes deepening. He looked back toward the shoreline, where the beach and caves loomed just beyond the fog.

"Listen, you'd best stay clear of those caves," he said, his tone low. "Tides rise fast, and fog can close in before you know it. Nothing good ever comes from poking around where you don't belong." Gigi tilted her head, giving him a polite but dismissive smile. Mr. Thornton's eyes narrowed slightly as he studied her, but he nodded.

"Don't take this lightly," Mr. Thornton continued, "And about that charge of yours. He must be somewhere around here; maybe he got cold and went to the cafe for a hot chocolate. That's what I'd have done in this weather if I didn't have a job I was coming from. If you're that set on finding him, fair enough. But mind yourself. Even the most careful folks can find trouble out there, especially when they don't expect it." He rowed them the last few feet to the dock and let her step out before he stood, gripping one oar tightly.

She stepped onto the dock, and just as she was about to turn, he spoke again. "And if you ever find yourself back here in town, the museum's worth a visit." His expression softened slightly. "I run it, in fact—plenty of history to learn, plenty of stories about the coast. Some might even interest a girl like you or be less trouble for that charge of yours."

Gigi flashed him a smile, already stepping away. "Thank you, Mr. Thornton."

He watched her for a moment, his eyes still shadowed with something she couldn't quite read, before he returned to his boat and started rowing away. As she walked back toward the shore, Gigi could still hear the steady creak of the oars behind her, fading into the mist. She pulled her coat tighter, feeling the dampness of the fog creeping in, but Mr. Thornton's warning lingered in her mind, adding a chill that went beyond the weather.

Chapter 3

Echoes of the Past

As she walked up the pier into town, the conversations she'd overheard and the symbols on the hull replayed in her mind, each detail sharpening her resolve. Willie was alive, and the compass in her pocket next to her trusty rope proved it. At least to her it did. She bit her lip. There was a secret here and she would find out the truth.

She was so lost in thought that she nearly collided with Mabel Simpson, the town's resident gossip, who was heading out of the general store with a basket of vegetables balanced on her hip.

"Goodness, child!" Mabel exclaimed, her eyes widening. She regained her composure quickly, peering at Gigi with a mixture of curiosity and suspicion. "What's got you so preoccupied this afternoon, hmm? I've seen you wandering around with that look in your eye. And where is that little charge of yours? Charlie, isn't it?

Gigi tried to shrug it off, but Mabel's gaze was relentless, pinning her down like a specimen under glass. "Up to something again, is he? That boy would keep anyone on the tips of their toes. You are a saint for taking him on. How did that happen anyway?

God knows it wasn't his mother that asked for it. She cares for little more than her Sears and Roebucks catalog, if you know what I mean."

Gigi nodded, not having a clue what the woman was getting on about, but knowing much better than to interrupt her. The words would double or triple if you tried to get one in edgewise with this woman.

"Now don't go asking if I've seen the little buggard." Mabel lifted up the hand not attached to the basket and held it palm out to stop the words Gigi was not going to say. "Or maybe you are less worried about that wayward boy and more concerned with what came in with the tide, eh?" Mabel's eyes gleamed as if she'd bitten into a perfectly cooked pastry.

She leaned in conspiratorially, her voice dropping to a hushed tone. "I know what you've been up to, Gigi. You're poking around that wreckage on the shore, aren't you?" Mabel's eyes glittered with something between amusement and a warning. "Looking for answers about your poor brother, may God bless and keep him."

Gigi stiffened. The last thing she wanted was for her investigation to become a talking point for every bridge club in Haven's Reach. She met Mabel's gaze, chin held high, and shrugged. Let Mabel figure this one out on her own. She was cold, wet, and in need of a scrubbing. But there was a little boy to track down. Gigi started walking away.

"Maybe, maybe not," Mabel said, tapping her chin thoughtfully. "But if you're planning on digging deeper, especially around Crooked Creek and that old lighthouse... well, maybe I ought to warn you."

Gigi stopped and turned back, despite her better judgment. Mabel gave a slow, theatrical nod, glancing around as if the secrets of the whole town rested on her shoulders.

"That lighthouse is bad news, Gigi. Always has been. And Mr. Kline—well, he's no friendly neighbor." Mabel shivered as if just saying his name gave her a chill. "They say he's a shaman, but I've heard he's a lot more than that. Communes with the devil. Knows things no one should know. That's why he stays out there by himself, keeping watch over Crooked Creek, scaring off anyone who dares to get close."

Gigi fidgeted with the rope in her pocket, her fingers tying and untying it with one hand. On her face, skepticism fought with intrigue. Mabel took that as a sign to continue talking—not that she needed one.

"Because he's hiding something," Mabel hissed, her voice barely above a whisper. She leaned even closer, her eyes wide with conviction. "He's got all kinds of strange herbs and potions. And those charms he leaves hanging in the trees by the lighthouse? Mark my words, they're not for decoration. Some people say he can curse you with just a look, and others..." She trailed off, glancing around to make sure they were alone, before lowering her voice to a whisper. "They say he talks to spirits."

Gigi's eyes widened, her fingers instinctively looping and twisting the rope in her hands, forming a bowline knot over and over again. The rhythm of the knot-making betrayed a flicker of doubt, but each precise twist and pull showed her undeniable interest, her hands moving even as her mind spun with questions.

"Yes, spirits. The kind you don't want to disturb," Mabel insisted, nodding vigorously. "People who've ignored his warnings tried to explore the lighthouse... well, they've come back with stories of strange noises, visions... like something didn't want them there. If they came back at all. And Mr. Kline? He always knows who's been snooping around, and let's just say he's not too forgiving."

Gigi's mind raced with questions and a fair dose of skepticism. Still, there was something about the lighthouse, about Mr. Kline, that had her instincts buzzing. Her hand kept automatically twisting the piece of rope she kept there, tying and untying the sailor's delight series of knots with practiced, one-handed precision. Each loop and pull seemed to mirror her swirling thoughts, her fingers moving faster as the mystery took hold of her.

Mabel seemed to notice the look in her eye, and she pursed her lips, shaking her head. "You listen here, Gigi. I know you're curious, and I know you loved your brother, but some things are better left alone. The Golden Anchor might be a mystery, but the Crooked Creek Lighthouse? That's a warning. Don't go looking for trouble with Mr. Kline."

Gigi's jaw tightened, her resolve strengthening under Mabel's warning.

Mabel huffed, her expression a mix of exasperation and worry. "I know that look. It's the same one your mama gets when I come over to chat on Sundays." Gigi's fingers grasped over the compass. The glass sliced into the pad of her index finger. She winced.

"Glad you feel the same way," Mabel hiked her basket farther up her hip. "Just remember: the sea keeps secrets for a reason, and so does that lighthouse. I've seen what happens to people who go looking for things they shouldn't." She leveled Gigi with a hard look. "And I'd hate for you to be next."

With that, Mabel turned and hurried off, casting one last wary glance over her shoulder, leaving Gigi alone with the chill of the morning air and a new mystery pulling at her thoughts. Gigi pushed the warning aside by pulling her hand out of her pocket. She still needed to find Charlie. The weather wasn't getting any warmer.

Gigi pushed open the heavy door of Porter's Café. The cafe wasn't far from the general store. The downtown itself wasn't much if you didn't count the Mill. Which everyone did, because without it, Haven's Reach would be little more than a native fishing village still. The comforting warmth hit her like a balm. The smells of cinnamon, coffee, and freshly baked bread folded around her like an old quilt. Outside, the fog draped Haven's Reach in a thick, ghostly shroud, muting every sound, but inside, a soft hum of conversation floated around the café, creating a small world separate from the sea and mist beyond its windows.

She paused just inside, gazing at the familiar faces tucked into their usual booths and stools at the counter. They glanced back—quick, furtive looks that darted away the moment her eyes met theirs. Gigi could almost feel the thoughts bouncing around the room, the unspoken condolences and sympathetic murmurs about her poor brother. The knowledge of the shipwreck had made its way through the town gossip line even as she was rowed to safety by Mr. Thornton.

Mrs. Belton, one of the local pillars of the community, sat next to her husband. He was a retired logger. One of the few. The two of them had made good money back in the day and now lived comfortably on Nob Hill, as Gigi's mother liked to call the large hill at the edge of town before the dunes. Mrs. Belton's eyes met Gigi's and then shifted, drifting toward the empty chair across the table as if imagining Willie sitting there. She leaned in close to her husband, muttering something behind her coffee cup. He shook his head, sneaking a glance at Gigi with an expression that seemed to echo the phrase "poor girl." Gigi's stomach twisted. She clenched her jaw, determined to shut them all out. They had already mourned Willie, buried him in their minds, leaving her as the foolish girl who couldn't let go.

She gave the crowd a quick, polite nod and then approached the corner booth, where Louisa waved, a steaming mug already waiting. Louisa wore a crooked smile, eyes wide with sympathy that she was careful not to overdo. Louisa knew better than to pity her friend.

"Saved you your spot," Louisa said as Gigi slid in.

The booth creaked as Gigi settled, her shoulders finally relaxing for the first time since she'd stepped inside.

"Thanks," she murmured. Her mama had raised her right. Thanking people was always the best thing to do, no matter the situation. Even little acts of kindness needed rewards.

Mrs. Porter, with her soft gray bun and quick, knowing eyes, appeared at the edge of the table, setting down a steaming mug topped with whipped cream and a generous sprinkle of marshmallows. She didn't say a word, just offered a gentle, fleeting smile before bustling back to the counter. Gigi didn't need to order; Mrs. Porter knew her well enough by now. Cocoa was her comfort drink, and Gigi suspected Mrs. Porter knew why she needed it.

Gigi wrapped her hands around the warm mug, letting the heat seep into her fingers, staving off the chill that seemed to cling to her ever since she'd seen the Golden Anchor's shattered remains washed up on the beach. She took a small sip, the sweetness melting over her tongue and, for a brief second, softening the ache lodged in her chest. The café's warm buzz faded into the background, drowned out by memories tugging at her thoughts.

Her eyes drifted to the frothy peaks of whipped cream, now dissolving into the hot cocoa. She remembered sitting here with Willie, laughing over mugs of cocoa after school. He'd always tried to sneak extra marshmallows from her cup when he thought she wasn't looking, grinning like a kid as he plopped them into his mug. He knew that they were her favorite. That was a brother for you, always taking the best for themselves. She would give anything to hear his laugh again, even if it meant no more marshmallows in her hot cocoa.

Gigi swirled the marshmallows with her spoon with a small sigh, watching them dissolve until nothing but soft wisps remained. That last visit together felt like a lifetime ago now. She grasped for details, searching for the exact color of his jacket and the sound of his voice, but they seemed to drift further away each time she tried, slipping through her mind like sand through her fingers.

She forced herself to take another sip, letting the warmth anchor her in the present. Gigi knew it wasn't just the cocoa she clung to—it was the last fragments of Willie she could still feel.

Louisa leaned forward, her voice low. "You've got the whole place buzzing, you know."

Gigi took another sip. The town folk had already decided about the shipwreck two years ago. She didn't care what sympathy they dared to offer now that it was real and not just promised.

Louisa's brow creased, her hand wrapping around her mug. "Look, I get it. But maybe…" She hesitated, glancing around to make sure no one was listening. "Maybe you're the one who needs to be careful. This whole thing with the Golden Anchor…"

Gigi's hand tightened on the mug to the point she could feel the burn from the heat. She could still see the wreckage, half-buried in the sand and twisted by the sea, as vivid in her mind as the first time she'd seen it. To her, it was not just a wreck. It was a message. Or a sign. Something from God telling her that her brother was still alive. She had proof this time.

Louisa searched her face, something softening in her expression. She nodded, reluctant but unwavering.

Gigi took a deep breath, the words catching in her throat. Part of her wanted to hold back and safely keep her hopes and fears away. But if there was anyone, she could tell; it was Louisa.

"Lou," she began slowly, eyes still focused on the mug in her hands, "I went down to the beach to clam with Charlie, but he wasn't there. What was there was wreckage. From the Golden Anchor." She looked up, searching Louisa's face for a reaction. "There were men, and I ran away, but then I found this..." Her voice wavered, slipping between excitement and something darker.

After a long pause, Louisa reached across the table, resting a hand over Gigi's. "Gigi... I know you want to believe that." Her voice was gentle but firm, grounding. "But everyone said the Golden Anchor went down in one of our worst storms. They searched for days, remember? They didn't find anyone. This is just what was left out there. It's finally coming home." Louisa took a long pull of her hot chocolate.

"As your best friend, I don't want you to get your hopes up."

Gigi flinched, a pang of frustration twisting in her chest. She tightened her grip on the mug, refusing to look away.

Louisa's expression softened further, her thumb tracing a small circle over Gigi's hand. "I know. And I know how much you miss him. But sometimes, not finding... closure doesn't mean there's still hope, Gigi. It just means..." She hesitated, choosing her words carefully. "It means the sea has its secrets."

Gigi bit her lip, looking away. Louisa's words stung, yet she couldn't help but hold onto her own belief, fragile as it was.

Gigi's eyes narrowed, a spark of defiance flaring up. She set her mug down, leaning forward as if she could force Louisa to understand with sheer willpower.

She hesitated, her gaze drifting as she felt a familiar ache tug at her heart. She could still see him on their last day together, standing on the pier's edge, the sunlight catching the red in his hair. He'd turned to her, his smile bright and carefree, and squeezed her hand. "I'll always come back for you, Gigi. No matter what." She'd laughed it off at the time, telling him he was being dramatic, but now, that promise echoed in her mind louder than all the doubts surrounding her since he'd disappeared.

Gigi set the compass on the table between them.

Louisa's eyes widened. "Where did you find this?" Gigi's long pause left no room for argument. Louisa looked to the left and right. There were only a couple of people in the cafe. The lunch rush was long over, and the dinner crowd had not yet arrived. But such a treasure shouldn't be left out in the open.

"The ship. Of course, you would be the one to find pirate treasure on a shipwreck." Louisa's hardened expression softened, the skepticism in her eyes giving way to reluctant understanding. She searched Gigi's face, seeing the pain and determination in every line. With a small sigh, Louisa reached across the table, taking Gigi's hand in her own, a silent promise of support.

"Alright," she said, her voice barely above a whisper. "I don't know where this will lead, but if it matters this much to you... I'll help. Just don't get your hopes too high, Gigi."

Gigi gave a slight, grateful nod, her resolve solidifying. She wasn't alone in this—not anymore. Together, they'd uncover whatever secrets the Golden Anchor held, no matter how long it took.

They must have been overheard because voices drifted from one of the only other filled tables in the room, soft but sharp enough to pierce Gigi's heart. She didn't even have to turn to know it was Mrs. Finch and Mrs. Bowers, each leaning in over their coffee cups, faces shadowed with the unmistakable look of well-intentioned pity.

"Such a sweet girl, but still holding on to that poor boy," Mrs. Finch whispered, a note of exasperated sympathy. "Sometimes you have to face reality for your good."

"It's been two years, Martha," Mrs. Bowers replied, her voice barely a murmur but heavy with finality. "She just can't let go, poor thing. Grief does strange things to the young."

Gigi's cheeks flared hot, her grip tightening on the edges of her cocoa mug. Every whispered word struck her like a stone, sinking into her skin and mind, lodging in her heart like a splinter. Let go? They wanted her to accept that he was gone—to give up hope just because they thought it was not very intelligent.

She set her mug down, the warm cocoa tasting bitter in her mouth, and clenched her jaw to keep herself from saying something she'd regret.

Louisa's hand brushed her arm, pulling Gigi's attention back to the table. Her friend had caught every word, the unspoken empathy in her expression saying more than any comforting words could.

"Forget them," Louisa murmured, leaning in so only Gigi could hear. "They don't know what it's like. And anyway," she continued, her eyes brightening with determination, "maybe you're right. Maybe you'll find something. But even if you don't... maybe looking will give you peace. It's worth it if it helps you, Gigi."

Gigi's heart swelled with gratitude, a sudden warmth cutting through the frustration. She met Louisa's gaze, and for the first time that morning, a small smile crept onto her face.

"Thanks," she said, her voice soft but steadier than before.

Gigi stirred her cocoa, the spoon moving in slow, absent circles as her thoughts drifted to a memory she hadn't touched in ages. She and Willie had been wandering the beach on one of those golden afternoons when the sun lingered in the sky slightly longer than usual. They'd stumbled upon strange, half-faded symbols carved into a driftwood washed ashore. With that sparkle of adventure in his eyes, Willie had called it "a message from the sea." He'd woven a tale about ancient sailors, lost treasure, and codes meant for only the cleverest to decipher. She remembered how they'd laughed, pressing their fingers into the grooves of the symbols as if they might spark to life under their touch.

Now, the memory made her shiver with realization. The Golden Anchor had washed up, broken, and beaten by the sea, but what if it held something more? What if those old symbols had been a sign? What if Willie had left something for her, hidden in the wreckage, just waiting to be found?

"Louisa," Gigi began, her voice edged with a renewed sense of urgency, "I think... I need to go back to the wreckage."

Louisa raised her eyebrows, her expression shifting between worry and cautious curiosity. "Gigi, you've already been there. What do you think you'll find?"

"I don't know," Gigi admitted, setting her spoon down and leaning in, her voice just above a whisper.

Louisa looked the compass over. "But I remember... You and Willie found these strange symbols on the beach once. He thought they meant something. What if... what if there's something like that in the wreckage? A clue, a sign... something he left behind?"

Louisa hesitated, "I'm coming with you," she said firmly. "If there's even a chance, I'll help you search every inch of that wreck."

A wave of gratitude washed over Gigi. Determined and united in their search for the truth, they decided to meet by the shore.

As she slid out of the booth, Gigi cast one last glance around the diner. Familiar faces and quiet conversations filled the space, and she caught a few curious looks from the same people who, moments earlier, had whispered about her "not letting go." That label might follow her, lingering on her shoulders as the mist clung to the coastline. But she pushed the thought aside, taking a breath and steeling herself. She was done caring about the whispers.

With a final nod to Louisa, Gigi stepped out into the fog, her mind sharp with purpose. Whatever waited out there, in the sand and wreckage, she was ready to find it. The townsfolk might think she was chasing ghosts, but Gigi knew better. She wasn't just searching for answers—she was searching for Willie, and no amount of fog or whispers could stop her. Now, if only tracking down Charlie was as easy. She looked at the clock on the wall to discover it was past dinner time. A colorful word from her father's friends popped into her mind. It would have to wait until tomorrow. Her coat was too wet to drudge any farther. Her own mother would worry and fuss over her if she didn't get home within the hour. There was nothing like the wrath of a logger's woman.

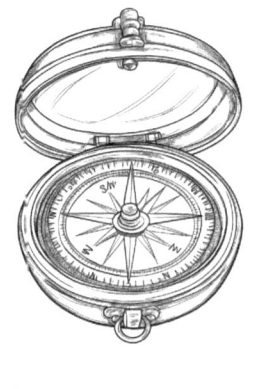

Chapter 4

Lighthouse Shadows

The next morning, Gigi stood at her bedroom window seeing nothing of the outside world as her mind churned over her plans. She pressed her palm against the cool glass to calm her racing thoughts. Today, she would seek out Mr. Kline, the reclusive shaman who held secrets of the land around the Crooked Creek Lighthouse—and maybe even of her missing brother, Willie. The thought made her pulse quicken in anticipation. She might be able to put closure on this for her family.

The murmur of conversation drifted from the kitchen, her mother's low, familiar hum mixing with the bubbling of something on the stove. Gigi recognized the smell instantly—kasha, simmering in a pot, as steady and reliable as the sunrise. Her stomach gurgled. Her punishment for being so late was dinner had been long devoured by the time she'd walked in the door. Her mother had ordered her to clean up and go straight to bed. They weren't about to waste lamp oil on a girl that couldn't watch the time.

"Gigi!" her mother called up the stairs. "Breakfast is almost ready. Your father has an early morning today; get up now if you want anything to eat."

Gigi slipped the small, rusted compass from her bedside table into her pocket. Her fingers brushed over its etched surface, tracing the strange symbols she'd found there the night before. They felt foreign, almost alive under her touch, but the metal's cool weight grounded her, reminding her of her purpose. Today, she would go to Mr. Kline, whatever that busybody had said. There were answers waiting, answers she needed to find.

When she entered the kitchen, her mother stood over the stove, spooning steaming kasha into bowls. Her father was seated at the table, already dressed for work, his coffee untouched as he read through the morning paper with furrowed brows. Her mother looked up as Gigi entered, her sharp gaze flicking over her, noticing, as always, more than Gigi wished she would.

"Gigi," a slight frown knitting her brow, "you were filthy when you came home last night. Covered in sand and saltwater. Just look at your nails," she added, gesturing with a hand still wrapped around the spoon. "What on earth were you doing?"

Gigi opened her mouth to brush it off, but her mother wasn't finished.

"And you know," she continued, ladling a spoonful of kasha into a bowl, "we're fresh out of clams for stew tonight. Your father and I had hoped..." She trailed off, giving Gigi a look that spoke more than words. Her mother had an uncanny way of knowing when something weighed on her, though she rarely pressed further. Today was no different. Her mother stopped just before pushing her over the edge.

Across the table, her father lowered the newspaper, his gaze steady and hard. "I don't want you poking around those cliffs, Gigi," he said, his voice holding a warning that sent a flicker of unease down her spine. "Or the caves. Or the lighthouse. You know better. Those forests aren't safe. They weren't safe for your brother and they are less safe for a girl."

Gigi fiddled with the rope in her pocket, looping it one way then another until a series of knots formed under her palm. "Papa, I—"

"No," he cut her off, his tone sharper than usual. He set down the newspaper and leaned forward, his hands clasped together. "I don't want to hear it. Your brother thought he was invincible, too, and look where it got him."

The room fell into a tense silence. Gigi's mother busied herself at the stove, her shoulders tense, her gaze firmly on the pot of kasha. Gigi looked at her father, feeling her throat tighten.

Gigi wanted to yell and scream back that it wasn't fair. She wanted to point out that it wasn't the caves or the lighthouse that got Willie in trouble; that it was him. Instead she took a calming breath. Mama was always talking about turning the other cheek. When it came to Papa, she was in the habit of doing it often.

"I say this for your own good," her father patted her on the cheek. It was supposed to be endearing. "I just don't want to see your mama cry again. You don't want to make her cry, do you, Gigi?" Her father's voice was softer now, a thread of pain woven through his words. He shook his head, his eyes dark and weary. "We've been through enough. Those places... they hold nothing but trouble."

Gigi's mother placed a bowl of kasha in front of her father, who gave her a brief nod of thanks. Her gaze lingered on Gigi, a faint crease of worry deepening between her brows.

"We just want you safe, Gigi," she said gently, resting a hand on her daughter's shoulder.

Gigi swallowed, looking down at her bowl, the warm steam curling into the air between them. She knew they were speaking out of fear, but something stronger, something unyielding, bubbled in her stomach. Her heart ached for answers, and her mind refused to let go of the strange symbols on the compass, or the shipwreck on the shore. She needed to know the truth—whatever it cost.

She picked up her spoon, trying to eat, though every mouthful tasted like paste and her stomach was already full. Her father rose, giving her a final, lingering look, one that held as much sorrow as it did warning.

"I'm trusting you, Gigi," he said, his voice rough as he donned his coat. "Don't betray that trust."

She nodded again, her face a careful mask of obedience, but her hand slipped into her pocket beneath the table, her fingers brushing over the cool metal of the compass. The etched symbols seemed to pulse under her touch, filling her with a sense of purpose that refused to be silenced. As her father gathered his things and left for work, the door closing behind him with a decisive click, Gigi's determination grew stronger.

When her mother's back was turned, Gigi pushed away from the table and slipped into her room. She grabbed her coat. The house felt oddly quiet in her father's absence, the usual warmth replaced by a chill that seemed to press her forward, urging her toward the lighthouse.

Her mother's voice called from the kitchen, faint and muffled. "Gigi, where are you off to?"

Gigi paused at the door, her hand tightening on the frame. "Charlie." It wasn't a lie exactly. She planned to go by the boy's house later to see why he'd missed their meetup.

Her mother's voice softened, carrying a hint of hope. "Promise to bring some clams if you're by the shore?"

Gigi sent a nod her mother's way, though her mind was already far from clams. She stepped out into the cool morning air, feeling the mist brush against her skin, the fog curling around her like a silent promise. She cast one last look at the house before heading down the winding path toward Mr. Kline's secluded cabin.

—

The trees loomed close as Gigi followed the narrow trail winding through the woods, her footsteps barely making a sound on the damp earth. Fog clung to the ground, swirling around her ankles, lending the forest an otherworldly quality that sent a thrill through her. This path was one she'd never dared to follow alone before; the adults in town warned children away from Mr. Kline's home, calling him a recluse, a man shrouded in mysteries better left unexplored.

But today, Gigi welcomed the unknown.

The closer she drew to the cabin, the more unsettling the surroundings became. Strange talismans dangled from tree branches made of bones. Feathers and twisted bits of driftwood rattling softly in the wind. A shiver ran down her spine as she caught sight of them, but she pressed on, driven by something she couldn't quite name. The path continued to twist and turn through the trees.

Finally, Mr. Kline's cabin emerged from the mist, a dark, weathered structure half-swallowed by the forest. Gigi took a deep breath, her hand slipping into her pocket to grip the compass for reassurance. She could feel the cold metal pressing against her skin, grounding her. She had come here to find out about her brother and nothing was going to deter her.

Raising a hand, Gigi knocked lightly on the door. The sound echoed, unnervingly loud in the otherwise silent woods. The door creaked open, revealing Mr. Kline—a tall, wiry man with piercing eyes that seemed to hold both knowledge and warning. His gaze settled on her, sharp and assessing, before his eyes flickered down to the small bulge in her pocket.

"I know why you're here," he said quietly, his voice rough as the bark on the trees surrounding them. "And I want you gone. Get off my property."

Gigi hesitated, a flicker of doubt gnawing at her resolve, but she forced herself to hold her ground. She reached into her pocket, drawing out the compass and holding it up, the strange symbols glinting faintly in the dim light.

Mr. Kline's expression darkened. His fingers twitched, but he didn't reach for it. Instead, he met her gaze with a look so intense it sent a chill down her spine.

"That compass isn't an old trinket," he murmured, his tone heavy with meaning. "It's a relic of a time better forgotten. It's tied to things better left alone."

Gigi swallowed, her mind flashing to the warnings from her father, the worry etched into her mother's face. But she couldn't back down now. She held the compass out a little farther, her voice steady despite her thudding heart.

"My brother," she started to say.

"Your brother was a fool; and so are you, girl, if you think that thing will help anyone. I know all about the ship in the harbor. Mark my words, Ships are worth money. Lots of money. Only a few profit from their demise." Mr. Kline's gaze flicked back to the compass, a flash of something unreadable crossing his face. "If you had any sense whatsoever you'd walk – no, run away from this place."

His words hung in the air between them. All Gigi had got up to this point was warnings. Don't do this, don't go there. She was tired of it. Why couldn't people share answers instead of cryptic words? When she made no move to run he stepped back, opening the door wider, allowing for her to enter.

"You'd better come inside," he said. "Stubborn, the lot of you. There are things you must understand, little Gigi. Things you won't like."

And despite the fear curling in her gut, Gigi followed him into the dark cabin, ready to face whatever truth awaited her.

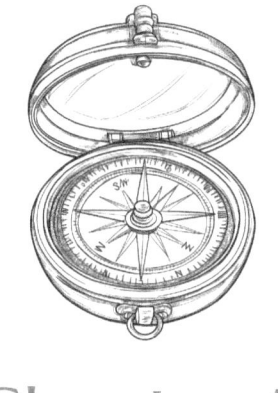

Chapter 5

The Secret Map

Inside the dim confines of Mr. Kline's cabin, the air felt thick, charged with a strange tension that prickled at Gigi's skin. The walls were cluttered with objects she barely recognized—jars filled with dried herbs, bundles of feathers tied with string, and small, carved stones that looked far older than anything she'd seen in Haven's Reach. A faint, smoky smell lingered in the room, earthy and sharp, like something rooted in ancient traditions.

Mr. Kline motioned her to a wooden chair near the table and lowered himself into his own seat opposite her, his gaze unwavering. Gigi felt the weight of his stare, like he was measuring her, trying to determine if she was strong enough for what he had to say. She set the compass on the table between them.

Mr. Kline's fingers hovered over it, his hand steady but hesitant, as if the small object commanded a power he both feared and respected. His eyes narrowed as he traced the symbols etched into the metal, his brow furrowing in concentration. Gigi watched him closely, noting the way his expression darkened, how the lines on his face deepened with each moment that passed. He muttered something under his breath—a phrase or maybe a word she couldn't quite catch. But his voice held a tension she hadn't heard before, a whisper of something old and dangerous.

Mr. Kline finally looked up, meeting Gigi's eyes with a somber gaze that seemed to hold layers of stories, each one darker than the last.

"These markings," he began, his voice a low rumble that made the hairs on the back of Gigi's neck rise, "are not just symbols. They are signatures—belonging to a group of pirates who once haunted these shores."

Gigi's breath caught. She'd grown up on the tales of pirates from her brother Willie, but those stories had always felt distant, like faded memories from another world. But the look in Mr. Kline's eyes told her that this wasn't just a legend to him. He spoke as if he'd known them, as if their presence still lingered.

"These men were ruthless," Mr. Kline continued, his fingers now barely skimming the surface of the compass. "Cunning and fearless, they sailed their ships into our coves under the cover of night. But unlike the pirates of your storybooks, they did not take to the seas for treasure alone. No, they had dealings with the people of this land—agreements that ran deeper than gold or silver."

Gigi leaned forward, captivated by the images forming in her mind: shadows slipping through the fog, weathered men exchanging whispers with locals under the cover of darkness. It was a world she could almost feel— raw and dangerous.

Mr. Kline's gaze sharpened, a flicker of something wary in his eyes. He glanced briefly toward the window, as if expecting someone—or something—to be lurking outside, listening. He quietly picked up a feather.

"Not trade as you'd know it," he replied, lowering his voice as if the walls themselves might betray their secrets. "These men didn't only want provisions or weapons. They sought knowledge—powerful, forbidden knowledge." A shiver ran down Gigi's spine.

Mr. Kline hesitated, his eyes drifting back to the compass. "These pirates believed that the spirits of the land and sea held power—a protection, if you will. They wanted this protection, wanted to be favored by the spirits to avoid storms, evade capture, and, some say, to keep death itself at bay." His fingers traced the edges of the symbols once more. "But power like that comes at a price."

Gigi's throat felt tight, her heart pounding as she hung on every word.

"Offerings," Mr. Kline said, his tone heavy with the weight of untold stories. "Some say they offered parts of themselves—blood, bone, even their names—to bind their spirits to the land. But other stories mention tokens, like this compass." His gaze bore into her, as if willing her to understand. "Objects imbued with pieces of their spirit, left behind as markers of their agreements, to keep them bound to this place. They thought it would make them invincible."

Gigi felt a chill settle over her, the kind that seeped into her bones and refused to let go. She looked down at the compass, the symbols somehow more sinister now, each one carrying a dark history, a connection to people who had vanished without a trace.

"You wonder what happened to them. I can see it in your eyes." Gigi didn't deny his words. She waited for him to continue the story. "Take this as a warning. Power like that corrupts. The best you can hope for is to not end up like them. They vanished," Mr. Kline moved his hands, making the feather he held there disappear like the men in his story. His tone remained flat, but his eyes held a flicker of something dark, something haunted. "Some say they sailed off into a storm that swallowed them whole. Others believe they were dragged beneath the waves by the very spirits they sought to control. But the truth, Gigi..." He paused, as if weighing his words carefully. "The truth is that no one knows. They left only their symbols, their tokens—objects like this compass. Cursed remnants of their dealings."

A silence settled between them, heavy and thick, like the mist outside pressing against the windows. Gigi's mind raced, piecing together fragments of Mr. Kline's story with the questions that had plagued her since she'd found the Golden Anchor's wreckage. Could the compass be connected to her brother's disappearance? Had Willie stumbled upon the same dark secrets that these pirates had chased?

Mr. Kline's gaze softened, a hint of pity in his eyes. "These symbols... they're not just decoration, Gigi. They're warnings. Traps, some say, to bind those who come too close. This compass, it isn't safe for you to carry. A good girl like you need not be mixed up in sinister things that this compass brings."

Gigi's hand moved instinctively toward the compass. She felt an odd sense of connection to it now, as if it held a piece of the truth she was searching for.

Mr. Kline's lips pressed into a thin line, his gaze growing darker. "That's the way of curses, Gigi. They don't always strike immediately. They wait... lie in shadows, biding their time. And when they strike, they strike deep." He leaned forward, his voice dropping to a harsh whisper. "If you continue down this path, you may not like what you find."

Gigi held his gaze, a mixture of fear and determination churning within her. She couldn't let fear stop her—not when she was so close to finding answers. "I don't believe in curses, Mr. Kline; only logic." And God. She couldn't leave God out. He was always with her. If Jesus couldn't protect her from a pirate curse, then who could?

"Logic?" Mr. Kline echoed, a hint of sorrow in his eyes. "You may seek logic, Gigi, but know that this land and sea have kept their secrets for centuries. Sometimes, what we call 'logic' is just the comfort we wrap ourselves in to avoid the truth."

He looked down at the compass once more, the flicker of a memory darkening his expression. "These pirates thought they could outsmart the spirits, thought they could gain protection by sacrificing a piece of themselves. But in the end, they vanished without a trace, leaving only their cursed relics behind." He gestured toward the compass, his eyes serious. "And those relics, they remember. They carry the echoes of those who came before, echoes that don't always stay quiet."

Gigi swallowed, feeling the weight of his words settle over her like the fog outside. But the more she listened, the more she felt an undeniable pull toward the lighthouse, toward the compass in her pocket. Fear and fascination warred within her, but curiosity was winning. Whatever secrets the compass held, they were connected to her brother, to the Golden Anchor, and maybe even to her missing charge Charlie. She would not give up on them, even if it meant that she'd be cursed.

Mr. Kline sighed, the fight draining from his face as he looked at her with something akin to resignation. "I can't stop you," he murmured, his voice laced with sadness. "But be careful, Gigi. The spirits don't take kindly to those who pry. And if you find yourself at the lighthouse... remember, not everything there will welcome you. Much like that charge of your's, Charlie, found out."

Gigi nodded, tucking the compass back into her pocket. She rose, the weight of Mr. Kline's latest warning lingering in her mind, but her determination growing stronger with each step she took. She didn't know what lay ahead, but she knew one thing for certain: she was going to find the truth, whatever it cost.

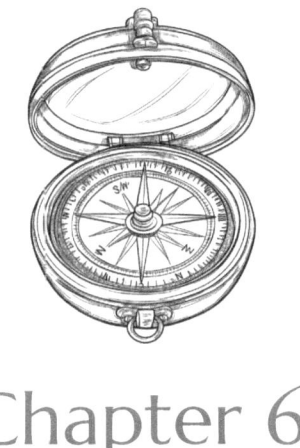

Chapter 6

Through the Storm

The late afternoon sun cast long, heavy shadows across Haven's Reach as Gigi made her way to Charlie's house, a sense of urgency propelling her forward. Fog drifted across the path, winding around her ankles like tendrils of smoke as she reached the narrow, weathered home where Charlie lived with his mother. The place seemed almost too quiet, as though it were holding its breath.

Gigi knocked, her hand hovering just a second longer, waiting for any sound inside. She didn't have to wait long; the door creaked open, and Mrs. Talbot's face appeared in the narrow crack, her eyes weary and rimmed with worry.

"Oh, Gigi," Mrs. Talbot sighed, her shoulders sagging as she recognized her visitor. "Please tell me you've seen him—Charlie's been gone since yesterday."

Gigi's heart dropped. She shook her head.

Mrs. Talbot opened the door wider, motioning for Gigi to come in. Inside, the house felt even quieter, as if Charlie's absence hung in the air, stretching out between the sparse furnishings making even this small space feel expansive. Mrs. Talbot wrung her hands, her fingers twisting together with nervous energy as she led Gigi into two chairs in the middle of the one-room house.

There was a double bed in one corner and a night stand next to it. A kettle lay in the fire, but no embers burned. Gigi hadn't spotted any cut wood outside, either. She made a mental note to tell her father. The church had a group of men that took care of the widows. With the winter season in full swing, the Talbots would need wood. It wouldn't take them too long to drop off a cord or two. Gigi stuck her tongue out, thinking. She had that pile of scraps her mom was always pushing her to make into a quilt. Maybe Mrs. Talbot could use them instead. Gigi wasn't much for sewing, and a quilt or two would really warm the space.

"I've searched everywhere I could think of," Mrs. Talbot continued, her voice trembling as she poured two cups of tea from the kettle.

The water was tepid, and the leaves provided little flavor. But Gigi sipped it anyway.

"I even went to the old pier, where he likes to fish. But he wasn't there. He's been talking about the Crooked Lighthouse for days, going on about some sort of treasure or 'secrets' he said he'd found." She paused, putting down her cup, the liquid untouched. She reached forward for the needle that sat on the edge of the table before looking at Gigi with pleading eyes. "You know how he is... always curious, always getting into trouble. If you see him, please... please bring him home."

Gigi nodded, her mind racing with what Mrs. Talbot had just told her. Charlie had mentioned the lighthouse. That was where she'd planned to go next. "I will," she promised, her voice steady with resolve.

Mrs. Talbot walked her to the door, but just as Gigi was about to leave, something on the ground caught her eye. Near the doorframe, half-hidden under a scattering of leaves, lay a crumpled piece of paper. Gigi bent down, picking it up carefully. It was a rough, almost frantic sketch of the Crooked Lighthouse, drawn with heavy lines, and surrounding it were strange symbols that looked oddly familiar. Next to the lighthouse at the base was the letter O and X. The X was larger than the O. Farther down the page were some scribblings; Gigi tried to make them out, turning the page this way and that.

"It's one of Charlie's drawings. Does one up any time I get him even the tiniest scrap of paper, he does." The woman was rambling at this point. Gigi kept looking at the paper, hoping to get some clue of what Charlie had been thinking.

Mrs. Talbot's face paled. "He's been drawing those symbols for days now. Said they were important. I thought it was just another one of his games... but now I don't know what to think."

Gigi folded the paper, slipping it into her pocket with the compass and her rope. She had seen symbols like these before, etched into the compass she'd found near the Golden

Anchor. Could it be a coincidence? Somehow, it didn't feel like one. But she kept her thoughts to herself, offering Mrs. Talbot a small, reassuring smile before heading back into the mist.

As Gigi made her way through the quiet town square, she spotted Louisa lingering outside the café, shifting her weight from one foot to the other, arms crossed. The fading evening light cast deep shadows across the cobbled streets, and the low murmur of the townsfolk's evening conversations was carried away by a brisk wind.

Gigi took a steadying breath, her hand slipping into her pocket to finger the crumpled drawing she'd found at Charlie's house. She felt the rough texture of the paper, the hastily drawn lines and symbols, and her pulse quickened. She'd memorized those markings, seen them before on the compass that had seemed to appear just for her. It was more than a coincidence.

Louisa's eyes narrowed the moment Gigi approached, and she raised an eyebrow, her skepticism practically radiating from her. "You've got that look again. Gigi, don't tell me. You're about to do something reckless."

Gigi's jaw tightened as she took another quick glance around, ensuring they wouldn't be overheard. She pulled out the paper, showing Louisa the symbols. She pulled the compass out too, allowing the other girl to examine both. A cold wind blew under their skirts. Gigi shivered.

Louisa took the paper lightly. "Where'd you get this? Charlie?" Gigi nodded.

"You found him?" Louisa asked excitedly. Gigi shook her head no. Louisa pursed her lips.

"Where do you think he went? The docks?" Gigi shook her head. "The lighthouse?" Gigi nodded.

Louisa held tighter to the paper, her fingers tracing the dark, hurried lines with a frown. For a moment, something flickered in her eyes—worry, maybe fear. But then she shook her head, a look of exasperation settling over her face. "So, what's your plan, Gigi? You're going to just march up to that creepy old lighthouse and hope something magically solves itself?"

Gigi shook her head sharper than she'd intended. She felt the surge of frustration bubbling up, the helplessness that had been growing since she'd found the wreckage.

"My mother is worried sick, and she doesn't want you getting tangled up in this mess, either," Louisa interrupted, crossing her arms tighter. "You're not a detective, Gigi! This isn't one of your little mysteries from last summer. You could actually get hurt out there!"

The accusation hit like a slap, and Gigi's cheeks flushed. She looked away, feeling the sting of Louisa's words settle deep. "Willie... Charlie..."

Louisa's mouth pressed into a thin line. "I care about you, Gigi. I don't want you disappearing into that fog like Willie, chasing some ghost of a clue. Those symbols? They could mean anything." She pressed the compass and the paper back into Gigi's hand. "Maybe Charlie was just messing around with stories or trying to scare himself. You don't have to risk everything over a drawing and a trinket."

Gigi's fists clenched. She glared at Louisa.

"Then go ahead," Louisa snapped, a flicker of hurt flashing in her eyes before she turned away. "You always have to be right, don't you?"

Gigi's breath caught, her resolve wavering. She hadn't meant to hurt Louisa, but she couldn't ignore the pull to the lighthouse, the insistent feeling that something dark and strange was waiting for her there. She looked at Louisa with pleading eyes.

Louisa faced her, her expression unreadable. "And if something happens to you? What then?"

"Then at least I'll have tried," Gigi finally whispered, her voice trembling. She looked down, gripping the drawing in her hand like a lifeline. "If my parents ask..."

Louisa exhaled, the fight draining from her face, replaced by a look of reluctant resignation. Her hand reached out, gripping Gigi's arm tightly. "I'll cover for you. I'll always cover for you. But if you go out there and anything feels off—*anything*—you leave. No staying out just because you're 'close' or 'might find something.' Promise me that much, Gigi."

Gigi swallowed, nodding despite the turmoil churning in her chest.

But as she walked away, leaving Louisa's worried gaze behind, Gigi felt a tremor of doubt creep in, like a shadow cast over her thoughts. She was doing the right thing. Her brother and Charlie needed her to solve this. That was the most important thing of all.

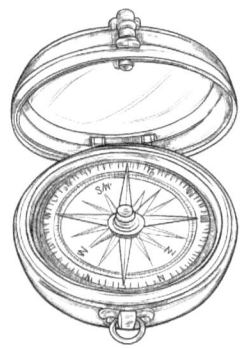

Chapter 7

Signs in the Sand

As dusk settled over Haven's Reach, Gigi slipped back into her home, moving quietly as she gathered her things—a flashlight, a pocketknife, and the compass. She could hear her mother in the kitchen, humming softly as she prepared dinner, blissfully unaware of the adventure her daughter was preparing for. With a final glance at her family, Gigi turned and crept out of the house, her heart pounding as she slipped into the misty night.

The fog was thicker now, curling around the narrow streets and casting an eerie glow under the streetlamps. Gigi made her way toward the cliffs, her footsteps muffled by the damp ground. But as she approached the edge of town, a prickling sensation crawled up her spine. The feeling of being watched was unmistakable.

She paused, scanning the shadows. Just beyond the reach of the nearest lamplight, a figure lingered—a tall shape cloaked in darkness, watching her with unsettling stillness. Gigi's heart raced, but she kept her expression neutral, refusing to let fear show. She took a step forward. The shadow man stayed put. Just a logger out smoking his pipe. She was getting jumpy. Gigi wound her way toward the cliffs. She kept her flashlight low, its narrow beam cutting only a small swath through the mist, but it was enough to catch movement—a dark shape slipping around the bend up ahead.

The figure paused, silhouetted for a brief moment in the fog, then shifted, slipping further into the shadows as if taunting her, daring her to give chase. Was it the same shadow she'd seen before? She couldn't tell anymore.

Determination flared up in Gigi, hot and fierce. She quickened her pace, her boots silent on the damp cobblestone. The figure moved faster, vanishing around the corner. Gigi broke into a light run, keeping her flashlight pointed forward, catching glimpses of dark fabric disappearing into the mist. Her pulse thrummed with a mixture of fear and exhilaration. She had to find out who was following her, why they were lurking in the fog, watching her every move.

As she rounded the next corner, her breath hitched. The street stretched out before her, empty. She was back in town. The shadow man had run her in a circle. No footsteps echoed back to her, no hint of movement stirred the dense mist. Gigi paused, catching her breath, fingers tightening instinctively around the compass in her pocket. The weight of it was both grounding and unsettling, a reminder of the strange symbols that connected this night to a long-forgotten past.

The silence pressed in, thick and heavy, as if the fog itself were holding its breath. Gigi strained her ears, listening for anything—a footfall, a whisper, even the creak of a door. But there was nothing, just the soft hum of the town, muted by the shroud of mist.

Suddenly, from somewhere to her left, she caught the faintest shuffle of footsteps. She whipped her head in that direction, flashlight darting through the fog, but the light revealed only more empty streets and the blurred outlines of the old iron lamp posts, their bulbs casting faint, sickly circles of light that barely pierced the haze.

Gigi's stomach knotted with unease, yet her curiosity propelled her forward. She pressed on, each step feeling more like a descent into the unknown, like she was following some dark thread that could unravel at any moment. She could feel the figure ahead, just out of sight, leading her deeper into the mist.

The street narrowed as she reached the outskirts of town, and suddenly, there it was again—the shadowed figure, only a few paces ahead. Gigi's breath caught as she caught a clearer look. It was tall, cloaked in something dark that hung heavily around its shoulders. The figure turned its head slightly, just enough that she could make out the suggestion of a face, though the features were hidden beneath the brim of a hat. A low chill trickled down Gigi's spine.

"Stop!" she called, her voice trembling with a mix of fear and defiance.

The figure tilted its head, almost as if acknowledging her. Then, without warning, it darted down a side path toward the cliffs.

Gigi hesitated, fear gnawing at her resolve. But she couldn't stop now; she needed answers, needed to know who was haunting her steps, keeping her from reaching the lighthouse and the answers it promised. Taking a deep breath, she plunged forward, feet pounding against the uneven ground as she chased the shadowy form through the swirling fog.

The path twisted sharply, the cliffs looming closer. The damp earth seemed to suck at her shoes, slowing her down, but Gigi pushed herself forward, her flashlight beam bobbing wildly as she navigated the narrow trail. The figure was ahead of her, barely visible now, slipping in and out of view as the fog thickened around them.

Just as she rounded a bend, a sharp crack echoed through the night—a footstep snapping a branch just ahead. Gigi froze, her heart hammering as she swept her flashlight over the trees lining the path. The figure was gone, vanished into the mist once again.

She stood still, her breath shallow, every nerve on edge. The eerie quiet settled over her once more, the fog pressing in so closely she could hardly see a foot in front of her. Gigi strained her ears, listening, waiting for any sign of the figure. But only silence stretched out before her.

Then, from somewhere behind her, came the faintest of whispers. It was impossible to tell if it was a voice carried in the breeze or a trick of her mind, but the sound sent a chill through her, tightening her grip on the flashlight. She spun around, the beam cutting a wide arc through the mist, but there was nothing—only the shifting shadows, twisting and melting into one another like specters.

The whispered words seemed to fade into the night, leaving her with a strange sense of unease. She took a steadying breath, pushing down the fear gnawing at her resolve. This shadowy figure—whoever they were—wanted her to feel this way, to leave her on edge, questioning every step forward. Gigi wouldn't let them win.

Squaring her shoulders, she turned back to the path, forcing herself to keep moving toward the lighthouse. With every step, the fog grew denser, as if it were alive, closing in around her, hiding whatever secrets the lighthouse held.

The ground beneath her turned rocky as she neared the cliffs, the faint outline of the Crooked Lighthouse finally coming into view. It loomed against the sky like a dark sentinel, its crooked shape casting long, jagged shadows through the fog. Gigi paused, taking in the eerie sight. The place felt ancient, forgotten by time, as if it held secrets too dark to share with the world.

A flash of movement caught her eye—a brief flicker of darkness shifting near the base of the lighthouse. Gigi's grip tightened on her flashlight as she stepped closer, scanning the shadows for any sign of the figure. The mist swirled around her, muting every sound, leaving her feeling isolated and vulnerable.

Then, just as she took a step forward, a voice—a low, unfamiliar voice—whispered her name.

"Gigi..."

The sound was barely more than a breath, carried on the night air, but it froze her in place. She swung her flashlight in the direction of the voice, her heart pounding as she strained to see through the fog. But once again, she found herself alone, the path empty, the figure gone as if it had never been there.

Gigi's pulse thundered in her ears, her thoughts racing. The fog, the voice, the figure—all of it felt like a twisted game, something designed to keep her off balance, to frighten her into turning back. But Gigi's resolve was stronger than her fear. Because true love casts out all fear. She had a mission to find her brother; what greater love was there than that between siblings? Whoever—or whatever—was haunting her steps would not stop her from uncovering the truth.

She turned back to the lighthouse, steeling herself as she made her way to the entrance. The door hung slightly ajar, creaking softly as the wind stirred it. She hesitated, fingers brushing over the compass in her pocket, feeling the symbols etched into the metal. They felt cold and foreign, almost as if they held a pulse of their own, urging her forward. It had been abandoned a while back. The town couldn't settle on one reason, but most of them came down to need and cost. So here it sat, empty.

Taking a steadying breath, Gigi pushed open the door and stepped inside, the darkness swallowing her whole as she crossed the threshold. The sound of her footsteps echoed off the stone walls, each one amplified, filling the space with an eerie rhythm. Shadows twisted along the walls, cast by her flashlight, creating shapes that seemed to dance and shift with every step.

The silence pressed in around her, thick and impenetrable, as if the lighthouse itself were holding its breath, waiting to see what she would do next. She took another step, her heart pounding, feeling the weight of every secret this place held.

And somewhere, just beyond her reach, the faintest whisper drifted through the air, taunting her.

"Gigi..."

She forced herself to keep moving, her flashlight casting long beams through the shadows, illuminating nothing but darkness.

The lighthouse's interior felt forgotten, a tomb left to rot by time. Dust lay thick over every surface, coating the cracked wooden floor, the rusted remnants of furniture, and the damp stone walls. But it was the walls themselves that drew her attention, her lantern casting an uncertain light on the strange shapes carved into the stone. Gigi moved closer, reaching out to trace her fingers over one of the etchings.

The symbols were rough, their lines jagged and worn from years of salt air and wind. She recognized them instantly; they matched the markings she'd seen on the compass she'd taken from the beach and on Charlie's drawing. Here, on the walls of the lighthouse, the symbols seemed to tell a story, each one linking to the next, flowing down the stone in an ancient script that felt as eerie as it was powerful.

A shiver crawled up her spine as her fingers moved from one symbol to the next. Some were familiar—a spiral, a crescent moon—but others were stranger, almost abstract, like twisted vines or distorted faces. Each line seemed alive, as if it could spring to life at any moment, whispering the secrets of a buried history.

Her gaze shifted along the wall, taking in more of the symbols, piecing together their possible meanings. The symbols seemed to grow darker, more ominous the higher they climbed, each one carved with purpose and precision that spoke of reverence—or fear. The air in the lighthouse felt heavier, tinged with a faint metallic scent that clung to the back of her throat, cold and unyielding. It made Gigi's stomach twist, a faint nausea spreading through her as she tried to decipher what each symbol might mean.

"Willie..." Gigi's voice was barely a whisper, a thought spoken aloud in the hope that he could somehow hear her. She felt a strange connection to these carvings, as though they were guiding her through his footsteps. Willie had known about these symbols; she could feel it. The patterns matched the drawings she'd found among his things, the hasty sketches he'd made in his notebook, as if he'd been mapping something out.

The lantern flickered, casting the shadows around her into a wild dance, and Gigi's pulse quickened as the air seemed to grow colder. She took a step back, her gaze darting around, half-expecting the dark figure from earlier to materialize beside her. But the room remained empty, the silence as thick as the fog outside, the shadows retreating once more into stillness.

A faint, eerie whisper drifted through the room, barely more than a breath, but it sent a chill down Gigi's spine. She strained to listen, every nerve on edge. The whisper was gone, swallowed by the silence, but it left an unsettling weight in her chest, a feeling that something—or someone—was watching.

She gripped the lantern tightly, her eyes sweeping over the carvings again. Toward the far side of the room, the symbols became more elaborate, sprawling across the walls in twisting patterns that drew her closer, as if the walls themselves were urging her to continue. She moved slowly, her heart pounding, each step drawing her deeper into the strange tale these markings seemed to tell.

The final symbol caught her attention, larger and more detailed than the rest, carved into the center of the back wall. It depicted a spiraling wave encircling a broken chain, surrounded by twisted vines and jagged lines that seemed to radiate outward like cracks in the stone. Gigi reached out, brushing her fingers over the pebbly surface, feeling the rough grooves.

A loud creak echoed through the room, startling her. She spun around, holding the lantern high, casting its light over the empty space behind her. Her heart raced as she scanned the shadows, searching for any sign of movement. The fog outside pressed against the windows, distorting the view. No one appeared.

As she turned back to the wall, something caught her eye—a glint, just above the final symbol. She leaned closer, squinting, and spotted what looked like a small metal plate embedded in the stone, almost hidden among the carvings. Gigi lifted her hand, brushing away the dust and grime, revealing an intricate design etched into the plate: a compass rose, with an arrow pointing sharply to the right, toward the door. Her heart rate spiked. It was as if the lighthouse itself was pointing her somewhere, the symbol showing her a path that led deeper into its secrets.

Following the compass's direction, Gigi turned, facing the narrow staircase that wound up to the top of the lighthouse. She hesitated, her breath shallow as she stared up into the darkness that stretched beyond her lantern's reach. The air grew colder, the faint scent of salt and rust thickening, the whispers in her mind growing louder, urging her onward. She steeled herself, clutching the compass in one hand and the lantern in the other, and began her ascent. Each step creaked beneath her weight, the sound echoing through the empty stone tower. The fog outside pressed in close, muffling the world beyond, trapping her in this strange place that seemed to draw her in.

The higher Gigi climbed, the stronger the smell of salt and decay became, mingling with a metallic tang that made her nose wrinkle. Her stomach twisted, but she pushed onward, her curiosity driving her forward despite the rising fear that gnawed at her thoughts.

Finally, she reached the top of the stairs, emerging onto a small, circular room with a single window overlooking the sea. The fog was so thick that she could barely make out the waves below, the endless, swirling mist casting the room in an eerie, gray light. Shadows clung to the walls, filling every corner, every crevice, as if they were alive, waiting for her to make the first move.

She stepped forward, her gaze sweeping the room, her senses on high alert. Her skin prickled, her heart racing as she scanned the space, searching for any hint of what had drawn her here. The carvings on the walls continued, more symbols etched into the stone, spiraling upward like a twisted mural.

And then, in the corner of the room, she saw it—a small bundle wrapped in faded, stained cloth. Gigi's heart pounded as she crouched down, her hands trembling as she reached for the bundle, feeling the rough fabric beneath her fingers.

Slowly, she unwrapped it, revealing a small, rusted compass with a cracked glass face, identical to the one she carried in her pocket. Her breath caught, and she glanced around the room, a creeping sense of dread settling over her as she realized she was not the first to stand here, to search for answers in the secrets of this forgotten lighthouse.

The air grew colder, a whisper brushing past her ear, and Gigi froze, clutching the compass tightly. She didn't dare move, didn't dare breathe, as the faint sound of footsteps echoed from the staircase below, slowly growing louder, approaching the room with a steady, relentless pace.

The lantern cast long, flickering shadows as Gigi crept through the narrow spiral staircase of the lighthouse. The thick, musty air smelled of salt and age, and every creak of the floor seemed amplified in the stillness. She moved slowly, each step carrying her further into the mystery, her heartbeat thrumming in time with the cold, rhythmic tap of the lantern against her leg.

As she reached the top, the small, circular room came into view, its walls adorned with carved symbols—some spiraling and twisting, others jagged and almost violent in their design. She ran her fingers over them, feeling their grooves, wondering what message they held, what secrets her brother might have seen here before he disappeared. The lantern's light caught on the final symbol, a broken chain encircled by a spiraling wave, and Gigi felt a strange, prickling sensation crawl up her spine.

A low voice cut through the silence, stopping her cold.

"Well, well, Gigi Levin. Couldn't resist, could you?"

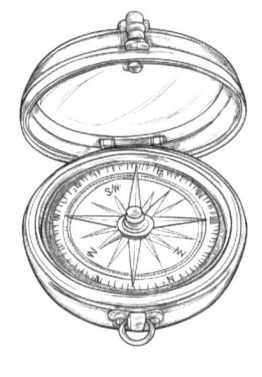

Chapter 8

The Hidden Door

Gigi whipped around, the lantern swinging wildly, its light casting frantic shadows. Standing in the doorway was Mr. Kline, his face shadowed but his eyes gleaming with a mixture of anger and something darker, something almost... pained.

"I...," Gigi stammered, trying to sound braver than she felt. "I need to know."

Mr. Kline's expression hardened. "I warned you. This place holds nothing but darkness, Gigi. You're meddling in things that should be left alone."

Before she could react, he crossed the room, his hand clamping down firmly on her shoulder. Gigi tried to twist away, but his grip was unyielding, his strength surprising.

"Let go of me!" she demanded, her voice trembling.

"We're leaving," he replied, his tone low and final. "Your father will hear about this. Perhaps he'll make you understand."

With a firm, relentless hold, Mr. Kline steered her out of the lighthouse, her protests muffled as the wind whipped around them, carrying the scent of salt and fog. The long, silent walk back to Haven's Reach felt heavy, each step weighed down by the dread curling in her stomach. Mr. Kline's jaw was set, his silence unbroken except for the occasional sideways glare.

When they arrived at Gigi's house, her father was waiting, his face drawn and tense as he took in the scene before him. Mr. Kline stepped forward, his tone clipped as he spoke.

"Mr. Levin, I found your daughter at the Crooked Lighthouse. She was... investigating. Despite my warnings."

Her father's face paled, then darkened, his mouth a thin line. He motioned Gigi inside, and she caught a glimmer of sadness in his eyes before it was replaced with stern resolve. Gigi's heart sank as she followed, dreading what was coming.

Once they were inside, her father closed the door behind them, his gaze steady, his voice calm but edged with steel.

"Gigi," he began, his voice low. "What on earth were you thinking?"

"I... I was trying to find answers, Papa," she replied, struggling to keep her voice from breaking.

Her father raised a hand, cutting her off. "And you thought you'd find those answers by wandering into that cursed lighthouse, sneaking around in the dark?" He shook his head, his face tight with anger and... fear. "You're risking more than you understand."

"But... Willie..."

Her father's expression hardened, his voice rising. "Enough, Gigi! You're young, you're stubborn, and you're chasing shadows that don't belong to you." He paused, a sadness clouding his eyes. "Willie... Willie is gone. And no amount of searching will bring him back."

The words hit Gigi like a punch to the gut, her breath catching as her father's words settled over her, cold and heavy. She could see the pain in his face, the way he'd tried to shield himself from hope, and it made her stomach twist.

"But what if there's something out there that could explain what happened?" she insisted, her voice breaking.

Her father's expression softened for a moment, but then he shook his head. "No more, Gigi. I won't allow it. I can't lose you, too. You are forbidden from going near that lighthouse again. Is that clear?"

Gigi's heart sank, but she could feel the determination bubbling just beneath her fear, like a fire that refused to be snuffed out. She nodded, barely meeting his gaze, knowing that he'd never understand why she couldn't let it go.

—

The night air felt thick and close as Gigi stormed down the quiet streets of Haven's Reach, her father's words still echoing in her mind: "You are forbidden from going near that lighthouse again." The memory of his stern, unyielding expression weighed heavily on her, mingling with the frustration simmering in her chest. Together they drove her to settle this once and for all. She'd climbed out her window and out into town. She gritted her teeth, her fingers curling into fists as she navigated the cobblestone path to Louisa's house, her only refuge in the midst of her father's anger.

When she reached Louisa's door, she barely had to knock before Louisa opened it, her eyes widening at the sight of Gigi's flushed cheeks and tense shoulders.

"Gigi, what on earth happened?" Louisa asked, ushering her inside without waiting for an answer. She led Gigi to the small kitchen at the back of the house, where the dim glow of a candle flickered on the counter. The faint scent of lavender hung in the air, and Gigi felt some of her anger begin to dissipate, replaced by a deep, aching need to vent.

Gigi dropped into one of the wooden chairs by the table, her face cradled in her hands as she struggled to find the right words. "My father..."

Louisa pulled out the chair beside her, resting a comforting hand on Gigi's arm. "I'm sorry, Gigi. But you know how parents are—they don't want to see the truth when it hurts too much. It's easier for them to believe in the worst than to have even a glimmer of hope." Louisa's eyes softened, her hand squeezing Gigi's arm gently. "But I know Willie meant everything to you. And I know you can't just give up."

Gigi nodded, her jaw tightening. She turned her head toward the lighthouse, almost willing it to be visible through the door.

Louisa's eyes sparkled with a mix of empathy and determination. "Your father said you can't go to the lighthouse, didn't he? Gigi nodded. "Then we go together. Secretly."

Gigi's head jerked up, surprise flickering across her face.

"Your father doesn't scare me," Louisa said, a mischievous smile creeping onto her face. "And I'm not about to let you go off on some dangerous quest without me. You think I'd actually sit back and let you have all the adventure?" Her voice softened, and she gave Gigi a firm look. "Besides, you're my best friend. And if Willie's out there somewhere, I want to help you find him."

Gigi felt a wave of relief wash over her, the warmth of Louisa's loyalty dissolving the heaviness in her chest. She managed a small smile, grateful beyond words.

Louisa leaned back in her chair, crossing her arms with a playful smirk. "You're welcome. Now, what's the plan?"

Gigi glanced around the room, her mind racing. The fog had grown thick outside, creating the perfect cover for a return trip to the lighthouse. Gigi held up her flashlight, her question unspoken.

Louisa's eyebrows shot up. "Tonight? Gigi, that sounds... a bit dangerous."

Gigi nodded, the memory sending a chill through her. She gave Louisa a knowing smile.

Louisa grinned, her eyes glinting with mischief. "You found something, didn't you?"

Gigi opened her hand, revealing the compass and Charlie's drawing. Louisa looked closely.

"Those symbols," she started. "Charlie drew them?" Gigi nodded. "But where did he…" Louisa looked at Gigi. "You found more, didn't you? In the lighthouse!"

Gigi nodded.

"Okay, tonight. My mother is asleep by nine on the dot, and I know every squeaky board in this house. I'll meet you by the path near the cliffs."

Gigi nodded, a weight lifting from her shoulders as their plan solidified.

The two friends shared a determined look, sealing their unspoken promise. Gigi felt a thrill run through her, part fear and part exhilaration, the gravity of their decision sinking in. Whatever they found tonight, they would face it together.

—

The fog was even thicker than before, swirling around the cliffside path as Gigi made her way toward the meeting spot. The familiar chill of the mist soaked into her clothes, clinging to her skin as she moved, her heart pounding with both anticipation and nerves. She clutched the compass tightly, its cold metal pressing against her palm as she waited for Louisa.

A moment later, Louisa appeared through the haze, carrying two lanterns. She handed one to Gigi with a nod, her expression serious but tinged with excitement. "Ready?"

Gigi nodded, gripping the lantern tightly as they started toward the lighthouse. The fog thickened as they neared, the sound of the ocean rumbling faintly in the background, a steady pulse that matched the thudding of her heart.

The Crooked Lighthouse loomed in the distance, its dark silhouette barely visible through the mist. As they approached, the building seemed to grow, its uneven shape casting eerie shadows across the ground. Gigi took a deep breath, the damp, salty air filling her lungs, grounding her. The lighthouse felt more alive tonight, its presence almost… watchful.

Louisa's voice broke the silence, a low whisper. "Are you sure about this, Gigi?"

Gigi nodded, keeping her gaze fixed on the lighthouse. She reached for Louisa's hand, giving it a reassuring squeeze. She looked her friend in the eye. "Stay close."

They moved forward, the lanterns casting pale yellow circles that danced over the stone walls. Gigi pushed open the door, and the same stale, metallic smell washed over them, filling the air with the faint scent of rust and salt. Louisa wrinkled her nose but said nothing, her grip on the lantern tightening as they stepped inside.

The carvings on the walls seemed even darker than before, their shapes twisting in the flickering light, casting strange shadows across the room. Gigi led the way, her fingers brushing over the symbols as she traced her path to the far wall, where she'd last seen the spiraling wave and broken chain.

Gigi paused, pointing to the final symbol. "This one... it's different. It feels like a warning."

Louisa stared at it, her eyes widening. "I don't like the look of it. Are you sure we should keep going?"

Gigi nodded, her gaze firm, her breathing steady.

They moved to the narrow staircase, each step creaking underfoot, the darkness pressing in as they climbed. Gigi's heart raced, her nerves tingling with a strange mix of dread and anticipation. The higher they climbed, the colder the air became, each step carrying them deeper into the unknown.

Finally they reached the top, stepping into the small, circular room that held the symbols' final secret. Shadows clung to every corner, the air thick with an almost tangible tension.

Louisa shivered, her voice a bare whisper. "What do you think we're going to find?"

Gigi raised her lantern, casting light over the floor. Her gaze locked on a small bundle in the corner of the room—a faded, tattered cloth tied around something. She stepped forward, her hands shaking as she knelt down, reaching for the bundle.

As she unwrapped it, a small, weathered notebook fell into her hands. She opened it slowly, her breath catching as she recognized the handwriting. Willie's handwriting. Notes, symbols, sketches—all things he'd discovered in his search for answers.

Louisa gasped, leaning over Gigi's shoulder. "This... this proves he was here."

Gigi's fingers traced the pages, her throat tightening as she took in each line, each frantic sketch that seemed to hold more questions than answers. But as she turned the pages, something caught her eye—a single line scrawled hastily in the margin, as if Willie had written it in a panic:

Some doors should never be opened.

The words settled heavily over them, a warning etched into the silence. And somewhere below, a faint creak echoed through the lighthouse, as if they weren't alone.

The hairs on the back of Gigi's neck prickled as the echo of the creak reverberated up the staircase. She and Louisa exchanged a glance, their eyes wide with fear and uncertainty. The words scribbled in Willi's notebook seemed to echo in her mind: *Some doors should never be opened.*

Another sound—a heavy, uneven footfall on the staircase below—snapped them into action. Gigi grabbed the lantern, snuffing out its light to leave them in near-darkness, her hand shaking as she clutched the notebook. Louisa's grip tightened on her arm, her breathing shallow as the footsteps drew closer.

"Gigi," Louisa whispered, her voice laced with panic. "We need to get out of here. Now."

Gigi nodded, feeling the urgency thrumming through her veins. She cast her gaze around the room, searching for any possible escape route. The faint light from the foggy sky outside illuminated the walls just enough to reveal a faint outline of a door hidden beneath layers of dust and grime. Her heart pounded as she pointed to it.

"There," she breathed, grabbing Louisa's hand and pulling her toward it. She brushed away the dust with her sleeve, revealing an old, rusted latch. Her fingers fumbled as she tried to pull it open, but it wouldn't budge. The footsteps grew louder, echoing ominously in the narrow stone stairwell.

Louisa's hands joined Gigi's, both of them tugging at the latch with a mixture of desperation and determination. Finally, with a loud creak, the door gave way, revealing a dark passage that smelled of salt and damp earth. Gigi's heart leapt—could this be some kind of hidden passage leading outside?

She rushed forward, dragging Louisa into the narrow space. She pulled the door shut behind them, their breaths mingling in the tight corridor as they pressed themselves against the cold, stone walls.

They held their breath, listening as the footsteps reached the top of the lighthouse. A shadow shifted under the crack of the door, lingering for a moment. Gigi's heart hammered, the fear coursing through her body like ice. Whoever was on the other side seemed to pause, as if sensing their presence, and then—after what felt like an eternity—the footsteps moved away, fading back down the staircase.

Gigi exhaled, the relief almost overwhelming. She looked to Louisa, her face barely visible in the dim light. She nodded away from the door.

Louisa nodded, her hand gripping Gigi's tightly as they ventured deeper into the dark passage. The air grew colder, and the scent of salt intensified, mixing with the earthy smell of damp rock. Their footsteps echoed softly, the only sound in the narrow corridor, until the passage began to slope downward, leading them further into the depths beneath the lighthouse.

The corridor twisted and turned, a maze of cold stone and salt-laden air, until they came to a small opening that led into a larger cavern. Gigi's lantern flickered back to life, casting a warm glow that revealed jagged rock walls covered in faint, worn symbols like those in the lighthouse above.

"We're in some kind of cave system," Louisa murmured, her voice a mix of awe and fear.

Gigi scanned the cave, her eyes landing on a narrow tunnel that seemed to lead further down. She pointed, a small smile of relief crossing her face.

They hurried forward, their footsteps quickening as the tunnel sloped even steeper, the air thick with the scent of saltwater and seaweed. But just as they were beginning to feel a sliver of relief, a noise echoed from behind them—a harsh, scraping sound, followed by heavy footsteps that sent chills down Gigi's spine.

"They're following us," Louisa hissed, her voice tight with fear.

Gigi gripped Louisa's hand tighter, her own heart pounding as they broke into a sprint, dodging low-hanging rocks and uneven patches of ground. The footsteps behind them grew louder, the sound bouncing off the cavern walls, making it impossible to tell how close their pursuer was. All Gigi knew was that they couldn't afford to slow down.

The tunnel began to widen, the walls opening up into a vast, echoing chamber lit faintly by the pale moonlight filtering through a narrow opening above. And there, at the far end of the cave, Gigi saw it—a large opening leading directly out onto the beach.

"Almost there!" Louisa gasped, gripping Gigi's hand as they sprinted toward the exit. The scent of the ocean grew stronger, the sound of crashing waves louder as they neared the opening.

Just as they reached the cave's mouth, a rough hand shot out of the darkness, grabbing Louisa's arm and yanking her back. She screamed, stumbling as the figure emerged from the shadows, his face hidden beneath a hood. Gigi whirled around, her lantern swinging wildly as she lunged at the man, the metal base connecting with his arm. He cursed, loosening his grip on Louisa just enough for her to break free.

"Run!" Gigi shouted, pushing Louisa toward the beach.

They burst out of the cave, the cold night air slamming into them as they stumbled onto the rocky shore. Gigi's eyes darted around, and her breath caught as she saw it—the dark, hulking silhouette of the Golden Anchor, its broken form resting against the sand, half-buried by the tides.

But they had no time to marvel or search the wreck. Behind them, the man's footsteps thundered closer, his angry shout echoing over the roar of the waves.

Gigi pulled Louisa toward a series of large rocks clustered near the base of the cliff. They scrambled over the rocks, crouching low as they squeezed between two large boulders, their breaths ragged and hearts pounding.

They waited, barely daring to breathe as the footsteps slowed, the man searching the beach. Gigi watched through a small gap between the rocks, her heart racing as he paced along the shoreline, his head turning in all directions, searching for any sign of them. After a tense few minutes, he finally turned, retreating back into the mouth of the cave.

Louisa slumped back, letting out a shaky breath. "That was... too close."

Gigi nodded, her gaze shifting to the wreckage of the Golden Anchor looming nearby. She could feel the pull of it, a strange, almost magnetic tug urging her to go closer.

Despite the lingering fear, she knew she couldn't leave without at least seeing it, without confirming that it was real. She tugged Louisa's sleeve.

Louisa's gaze followed hers, and she took a deep, steadying breath. "Do you want to... look inside?"

Gigi nodded, a grim determination settling over her. Together, they crept from their hiding spot, the sand cold and damp beneath their feet as they approached the wreck. The hull of the Golden Anchor was cracked and weathered, its wood swollen and splintered from the relentless battering of the sea.

They climbed onto the deck, their movements slow and cautious as they navigated the creaking boards. The ship's interior was a haunting mix of shadows and twisted metal, the remains of its former life preserved in eerie silence. Gigi's heart ached as she imagined her brother here, moving through these same halls, perhaps chasing the same secrets that now consumed her.

Near the captain's quarters, she noticed something glinting in the pale moonlight—a silver pocket watch, its face cracked, resting on the floor. Gigi's breath caught as she picked it up, her fingers brushing over the initials carved into the back: *W.L.* Her heart clenched, a bittersweet wave of grief and hope flooding through her.

"Willie," she whispered, her voice breaking.

But before she could say anything else, a sharp cry echoed across the beach. The man had returned, his silhouette emerging from the cave entrance. He spotted them, his shout carrying over the crashing waves as he charged toward the ship.

"Go!" Louisa yelled, grabbing Gigi's arm and pulling her back toward the rocks. They scrambled over the jagged edges, their hands and knees scraping against the rough stone as they fled, Gigi clutching the pocket watch tightly in her hand.

As they reached the far end of the beach, hidden by the shadows of the cliffs, Gigi risked a glance back. The man stood on the deck of the Golden Anchor, his figure dark against the night sky, his posture tense as he scanned the beach.

They slipped away, their breaths coming in shallow gasps as they made their way back up the path to town. Gigi's heart raced with both fear and a strange sense of victory. She had something of Willie's, a piece of him that felt like a sign, a clue to the mystery that had begun to unfold.

But they had barely escaped with it. And as they hurried back toward the safety of town, Gigi knew that the man in the cave wouldn't stop hunting them down.

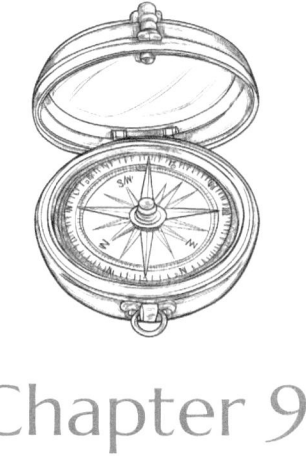

Chapter 9

The Tide of Truth

As Gigi made her way through Haven's Reach, her mind was as thick with questions as the morning's fog had been. Her thoughts darted back to the discoveries she and Louisa had made in the lighthouse. She had barely slept, her dreams filled with shadowy figures and the relentless sound of waves crashing against rocks. Now, as she moved through the town square, that uneasy feeling refused to fade.

A group of men lingered near the edge of town, their dark coats and rough faces unfamiliar. Gigi paused, glancing over them with a frown. They were gathered near the general store, speaking in low voices, each casting wary glances toward passersby. She had never seen them before, and in a town as small as Haven's Reach, newcomers didn't go unnoticed. It struck her that, despite their attempts to look like loggers, they wore tattered boots and old-fashioned coats that seemed more suited to the sea than to the forest.

Gigi slowed, pretending to examine a rack of souvenirs. But her attention wasn't on the trinkets; it was riveted to the two women in animated conversation nearby. Mabel, the self-proclaimed keeper of the town's secrets, leaned in close to Mrs. Belton, the sturdy and no-nonsense wife of a local logger.

"...and I'm telling you, I've never seen them before," Mabel whispered conspiratorially, her eyes darting around to make sure they weren't overheard. "Three of them, rough around the edges. Showed up at the mill claiming they were hired on, but no one knows a thing about them. And they've got that look about them, you know?"

Mrs. Belton's brow furrowed as she nodded. "I noticed that too. They don't carry themselves like the usual mill workers. Logan said one of them had hands more calloused from ropes than an ax, and the way they watch people—well, it's not right."

A chill prickled at the back of Gigi's neck. She kept her eyes on a garish shell necklace but leaned just a fraction closer, her heartbeat quickening. The Golden Anchor wreck had been the talk of the town since it ran aground a few weeks ago, its cargo mysteriously missing. Ever since, she'd had a feeling something—or someone—was lying in wait. Could these strange men be involved?

She forced herself to turn away, acting as if she'd lost interest in the trinkets. Her mind, though, spun with questions. It was true that timber was booming here, but these men...no, they weren't here for lumber. They had that wary, searching gaze of sailors who'd seen more than the rolling surf.

When she rounded the corner toward the café, she spotted Louisa waiting outside, her gaze darting nervously around. Gigi quickened her pace, took her friend by the arm, and marched her into the safety of the cafe. Together they slipped into the booth where they were less likely to be overheard. The cafe was buzzing with its normal morning traffic. Mostly cookless loggers and mill workers that bunked in the local bunkhouses. All unmarried gruff men who cared more about filling their bellies than listening to two jobless girls talk about other men.

"Gigi, have you seen the new guys around town?" Louisa whispered as she slid into the seat. "I passed them on my way here—they're by the general store, trying to look like loggers, but..." she trailed off, glancing toward the window where a few of the strangers still lingered.

Louisa's eyes widened as she leaned in. "I noticed them yesterday. I think there's more than just those few. I saw at least three near the pier earlier." She hesitated, lowering her voice even more. "They don't look like the usual lumber crew. It's almost like they're... watching something."

Gigi nodded, her mind racing.

"If they're not loggers," Louisa continued, "they might be here for the Golden Anchor." She shuddered. "Do you think these could be the same people involved with... whatever happened to Willie?"

The thought made Gigi's heart tighten. She'd hoped her brother's disappearance was a tragic accident, something that didn't involve any ill intentions. But with each new clue, each strange figure she encountered, the idea that he'd been tangled in something darker grew harder to dismiss.

"If they are," Louisa said, "Do you think they'll follow us? I mean, after last night at the lighthouse... They wouldn't risk us finding anything they want hidden."

Gigi nodded, glancing over her shoulder, her face set with determination.

Louisa sighed. "Then we just have to keep our eyes open. They're scary, but if they're connected to Willie, we should get to the bottom of it."

Gigi smiled as their cocoa was delivered. She wrapped her hands around the mug, basking in its warmth. She took a sip, the rich sweetness grounding her.

"I still can't believe we found the Golden Anchor," Louisa said excitedly. "That ship... it's just sitting there on the beach like it's waiting for someone to discover its secrets. And Willie's pocket watch?" She let out a low whistle. "Gigi, that's... well, I don't even know what that is. It's both amazing and terrifying."

Gigi reached into her bag, pulling out Willie's notebook and the compass, laying them on the table between them. She traced her fingers around the symbols, deep in thought.

"There has to be a reason Willie was drawn to these symbols," Louisa said. She leaned forward, her eyes narrowing as she studied the objects. She picked up the notebook, thumbing through the worn pages, her brow furrowing. "Look at these sketches. He's copied the symbols down carefully, but some of them look different from what we saw in the lighthouse. See these jagged lines here?" She traced a finger over one of Willie's drawings. "They're... almost angry, if that makes any sense."

Gigi nodded, her gaze shifting to the compass. She picked it up, studying the etchings on its frame, trying to see something she'd missed before.

Louisa tilted her head, staring at the compass with a mixture of fascination and frustration. "This compass... if it's a key, like the man said, then what's it unlocking? A place? A message?" She let out a sigh, her fingers tapping on the table. "And why would Willie have gone to such lengths to find it?"

Gigi flipped through the notebook, her fingers brushing over her brother's familiar handwriting, feeling both closer to him and more confused than ever. The symbols didn't look random. They were specific, intentional. They had to mean something. She paused, thinking of Mr. Kline's warnings, the way he had spoken about the lighthouse and the curses etched into its walls. But a nagging distrust tugged at her. He was hiding something; she just didn't know what.

Louisa nodded slowly, her gaze sharpening. "Have you thought about the museum?"

Gigi glanced at her friend, eyebrows raised.

Louisa nodded, her voice thoughtful. "You know, the history museum just down the road. It's filled with stuff from Haven's Reach—artifacts, old maps, books. There's bound to be something there that could explain the symbols. And if it doesn't, at least you might learn more about the lighthouse or any old myths about the area."

Gigi chewed on her lip, considering it.

"The curator, Mr. Thornton... he's always been nice enough," Louisa said. "He might even let us look through some of the archives if we ask. And you know Mr. Thornton is a bit of a history nut. He'd probably love to talk your ear off if you just tell him you're researching some 'historical project.'"

A small smile tugged at Gigi's lips. Gigi felt a wave of gratitude wash over her. She reached across the table, squeezing Louisa's hand. "Thank you, Lou."

Louisa shrugged, but her eyes shone with loyalty. "I'm in it as long as you are. So, are we going to the museum after this?"

Gigi nodded, tucking Willie's notebook and the compass back into her bag.

They finished their hot chocolate, nerves steadying as their plan took shape. Gigi felt a renewed determination settle over her; this mystery wouldn't unravel easily, but with each clue, each step forward, she felt closer to the truth—and to her brother.

As Gigi slid out of the booth, she felt a pang of guilt tugging at her. She hadn't just promised herself to get closer to Willie's trail that day; she'd also promised her mother she'd bring clams home for dinner. It was a small task, but the way her mother's eyes had softened when she'd asked made it feel important, grounding.

She glanced at Louisa "Listen, once we're done at the museum... would you mind if we went clamming down by the shore?"

Louisa raised an eyebrow, a small smile creeping onto her face. "Your mom ask for clams again?"

Gigi nodded, grinning.

Louisa chuckled, slinging her bag over her shoulder. "Fine by me. Let's get our mystery-solving out of the way first, then we'll get our hands dirty."

With a plan in place, the girls headed to the museum, the brisk autumn air clearing their heads as they walked.

Chapter 10

Uncharted Waters

The museum sat near the edge of town, a modest two-story building made of weathered stone. A faded sign with "Haven's Reach Historical Museum" etched in peeling gold lettering hung above the door. Inside, the air was tinged with the faint smell of old books and polished wood, a place steeped in memories and history.

The girls found Mr. Thornton behind the front desk, peering through a magnifying glass at a dusty old map. The curator looked up, adjusting his glasses with a curious smile as they approached.

"Well, if it isn't Gigi Levin and Louisa Roberts," he said warmly. "What brings you two here? I don't often see young people haunting these halls."

Louisa cleared her throat, keeping her tone casual. "Actually, Mr. Thornton, we were hoping to look into some old symbols. You know, for a... history project. We were wondering if you have any records of markings associated with old ships or local legends?"

Mr. Thornton's eyebrows shot up with interest. "Ah, Haven's Reach has plenty of legends, all right. And old markings? You've come to the right place. I'll take you to the archives."

They followed Mr. Thornton down a narrow hallway and through a door into a cramped room filled with shelves crammed with dusty books, boxes, and binders stuffed with yellowing papers. He led them to a corner and pulled out a hefty tome labeled "Nautical Symbols of the Northwest Coast."

"This book here covers symbols used by mariners, explorers, and, yes, even a few pirates who once prowled our shores," he said, placing the book reverently on the table. "And over here—" he pointed to a drawer with a delicate brass handle, "—you'll find some sketches from local lore. They're rough, but they may help you with that project of yours."

"Thank you, Mr. Thornton," Louisa said.

Gigi's heart pounding with a mix of excitement and anxiety. The girls exchanged a look before opening the book, their eyes scanning the old pages for anything that might match the symbols from the lighthouse and Willie's notebook.

An hour passed in a blur of flipping pages, squinting at faded drawings, and muttering about what might be a clue or just another legend. The compass, the symbols, the strange connections between the lighthouse and the old wreckage—it was all there in fragments, hints of a story that was too tangled to make sense of on their own. The book held no concrete answers, just possibilities that deepened the mystery.

Frustrated but determined, Gigi glanced at Louisa, who looked equally overwhelmed.

"It feels like every time we find a clue, we get three new questions," Louisa said. She then gave a half-smile, nodding. "But at least we know there's something there. It's like the mystery's alive, just waiting for us to uncover it."

They thanked Mr. Thornton and headed back into the crisp afternoon. As the weight of the museum's mysteries settled in their minds, Gigi felt a sudden pull back to the present, to her promise.

"Well, let's go find those clams," Louisa said, a smile tugging at her lips. "I can already hear your mom asking where they are."

They made their way down to the beach, where the low tide exposed stretches of damp sand and clusters of rocks dotted with tiny pools. Gigi handed Louisa a small bucket and a digging spade, and they set to work, wading through shallow waters as they scanned the sand for any signs of clams.

Gigi knelt down, pushing her spade into the sand, feeling the satisfying scrape as she unearthed a few shell fragments. She scooped up a decent-sized clam, tossing it into her bucket with a grin.

Louisa laughed, pulling up her own handful of clams. "This is definitely safer than dodging shadowy men and climbing around in haunted lighthouses."

They continued to dig, the repetitive rhythm of clamming bringing a strange calm to the afternoon.

"Do you think we're actually getting closer to something?" Louisa asked, glancing at Gigi as she held up another clam.

Gigi nodded.

Louisa shrugged, wiping sand from her hands. "Maybe. Maybe not. But we're closer than we were yesterday, and that's something. Plus, it feels... real. Like there's something waiting for us to uncover."

Gigi felt a swell of gratitude for her friend, for her steady presence in all this uncertainty. They'd uncovered fragments of the mystery and even made small progress, but they still had a long way to go.

The sun was sinking toward the horizon by the time they had filled their buckets with clams, the light casting golden reflections on the water. Gigi held up her bucket with a satisfied grin.

Louisa chuckled, giving Gigi's bucket a quick shake. "I think your mom will be proud of her daughter's foraging skills. Now let's get back and see if she makes that stew of hers."

With a final look at the beach, Gigi felt a sense of renewed determination. This might be just a clamming trip, but it was also a reminder of why she was doing this—to bring her brother back, to finally know the truth. And for the first time since their search began, she felt the tiniest glimmer of hope.

It was a few days before Gigi and Louisa could break away from their chores to continue the hunt. Gigi's mom had been extra needy with the laundry and cooking. Not that she let Gigi anywhere near the family's dinners.

"You have other gifts," her mom had told her. "And God will help you find how to put them to good use one of these days."

Even though she was past school age, Gigi had yet to secure a job. The mill didn't bring on women, and there wasn't much else in town. Watching Charlie had at least filled time, but with him missing there was little to do outside the house in the way of regular work. But somehow her mom had made that work take up a whole two days.

She was lucky that her mom had let her break away today to get some staples from the general store. Gigi decided to pay a visit to Mr. Thornton at the museum before picking up what her mother needed. If there was anyone in Haven's Reach who might know something about strangers and their connections to the past, it was him. She and Louisa reached the museum as the last of the morning fog lifted, leaving the town bathed in a thin, pale light.

Inside, the quiet hum of the museum seemed almost comforting, a sharp contrast to the unease outside. Mr. Thornton was at his usual post, carefully cataloging a series of ancient maps spread across the counter. He looked up as they approached, his expression softening with a welcoming smile.

"Well, if it isn't Gigi and Louisa. I take it you're here to dig a little deeper into Haven's past?"

Gigi smiled, nodding as she approached the counter.

"We were hoping you might help us," Louisa said. "We've been... well, let's just say we're noticing some strange things in town lately."

Mr. Thornton raised an eyebrow, the hint of a knowing smile playing on his lips. "Strange things, you say? I wouldn't be surprised. Haven's Reach has always been a place for strange things, if you know where to look."

Louisa leaned forward, her curiosity obvious. "We were wondering if you've noticed the new men around town. They don't exactly look like loggers. They seem more like sailors—or maybe smugglers."

Mr. Thornton's smile faded, and he cast a wary glance toward the door before lowering his voice. "I have noticed them, yes. Strange group, that one. Not many of us have crossed paths with them directly, but I've heard enough to know they aren't the usual crew we see in town."

Gigi felt a spark of hope.

"Do you know anything about them?" Louisa continued. "Or... about the lighthouse?"

Mr. Thornton's gaze shifted, a flicker of caution in his eyes. "The lighthouse has always been a point of interest, especially for those with secrets to keep. It's secluded enough to avoid prying eyes, yet close enough to the coast to be convenient for... certain types of business."

Louisa shot Gigi a look, the same thought clearly crossing her mind. "What kind of business?" Louisa asked.

Mr. Thornton swallowed. "It's fairly simple to transfer things from one point to another. And some might want to do so away from prying eyes."

"You mean smuggling?" Louisa asked.

Mr. Thornton lowered his voice. "That's a word for that kind of business, yes."

"And are there... certain types of people here who might be involved in that kind of business?"

Mr. Thornton sighed, leaning against the counter with a weary look. "Look, girls, it's no secret that Haven's Reach has had its fair share of questionable characters. Some of those people come and go, others stay. But if you're asking if some of our own townsfolk have ever... crossed lines, well, let's just say I wouldn't be surprised."

He leaned in, his voice barely more than a whisper. "And watch for those who always seem to know everyone's business. Information can be as valuable as any treasure, you know."

Gigi's thoughts immediately drifted to Mabel Simpson, the town's resident gossip. Mabel knew everyone's business, every secret, every rumor that passed through the town. She was the type to know things before they happened, and she thrived on having something to whisper about. Gigi had always brushed her off as harmless, but now the woman's nosiness took on a more sinister light.

As if reading her thoughts, Mr. Thornton nodded. "Mabel's a sharp one. People assume she's harmless because she's got a talent for small talk and a knack for knowing everything. But you'd do well to watch her closely. Sometimes the ones who seem the least threatening can be the ones holding all the cards."

Louisa's mouth fell open, her eyes wide with surprise. "You think Mabel could be involved with the smugglers?"

Mr. Thornton gave a small, cryptic smile. "Let's just say I wouldn't underestimate her, girls. And I'd keep your eyes open around her."

They left the museum with a new layer to the mystery. Gigi's mind was spinning as they walked down the road, Louisa by her side, both lost in thought.

"Mabel," Louisa murmured, shaking her head. "She's just so... gossipy. Why would she be involved in something this dark?"

Gigi's eyes darkened.

"Well, maybe that's why," Louisa continued. "She knows what everyone's up to, so it wouldn't be hard for her to play both sides. If the smugglers needed information, she'd have it. And if she needed to keep them quiet, she'd have the leverage." She shivered. "So, who do we trust? It feels like anyone could be part of this."

Gigi squared her shoulders, determination burning in her chest.

Louisa sighed. "I know; we keep following the clues and watching everyone, especially Mabel. If she's part of this, she'll slip up. People like her always do."

Chapter 11

Secrets Beneath the Surface

The next few days passed with Gigi and Louisa keeping careful tabs on both Mabel and the new men in town. Gigi noticed how Mabel's friendly smile lingered a bit too long on the strangers, how she always seemed to be talking to them, sharing a word here, a whisper there. Her gestures were animated, overly friendly—almost as if she was trying to keep them at ease.

One morning, while passing the pier, Gigi spotted Mabel chatting with one of the newcomers. He looked uneasy, casting nervous glances over his shoulder as Mabel leaned in, speaking in a low, confidential tone. The man eventually walked off, looking tense, while Mabel lingered a moment, watching him disappear into the fog with a satisfied smirk.

"That's it," Louisa whispered to Gigi; she had joined her in watching the scene unfold. "We have to find out what she's telling them. And why they're so nervous around her.

But how?" She bit her lip. "If she's as smart as Mr. Thornton says, she'll know if we're following her."

Gigi's mind raced, her gaze still fixed on Mabel's retreating form. She gave Louisa a knowing look.

"We have to stay close without being seen," Louisa said. "Tonight, let's stake out her house. If she's involved with the smugglers, she's bound to make contact with them."

That evening, as the fog rolled in thick over Haven's Reach, Gigi and Louisa hid themselves behind the tall hedges across from Mabel's small house. The two girls watched, breaths shallow as they scanned the quiet street for any sign of movement. Gigi stifled a yawn, beginning to wonder if their theory about Mabel was just wild speculation. But then, as if on cue, the front door creaked open. Mabel stepped out, glancing up and down the street before hurrying off in the direction of the pier, her steps quick and purposeful.

Gigi nudged Louisa, her heart racing as they trailed after Mabel, keeping to the shadows, careful to stay far enough back that they wouldn't be seen. They watched as she reached the pier, stopping near a cluster of boats. A dark figure appeared, stepping out from behind one of the posts, and approached her.

Louisa's eyes widened. "That's one of the strangers, Gigi. She really is meeting them."

The two girls watched as Mabel spoke to the man, gesturing toward the horizon, her voice low. The man nodded, handing her a small, dark bundle that she tucked away with a quick, furtive glance around. Mabel looked satisfied as she slipped back down the pier, heading toward her house.

When she'd disappeared from view, Louisa turned to Gigi, her face pale with shock. "It's true. Mabel's involved with them, just like we thought. What do you think they gave her?"

Gigi shook her head, her mind racing with possibilities.

"Gold? Jewels?" Louisa asked. "Maybe payment for helping them?"

They exchanged a look of grim determination, the gravity of their discovery settling over them. Their suspicions had been right, but that knowledge felt dangerous now, like they'd crossed a line they couldn't uncross. If Mabel was involved with the smugglers, who else could be?

But Gigi knew one thing for certain: they had to keep digging. She'd find the truth about her brother, no matter who stood in her way.

Gigi and Louisa sat huddled together in Gigi's small room, their heads bent over Willie's worn journal, its pages now filled with clues that seemed to pulse with a strange life of their own. Gigi traced her fingers over her brother's careful, looping handwriting, trying to make sense of the symbols she and Louisa had uncovered over the past few days.

The journal, usually a comfort, felt different tonight. With each new entry they deciphered, the mystery grew, the pieces falling into place, but forming a picture she didn't yet understand. Willie's notes were written in fragments, a mix of sketches, symbols, and hastily jotted words that gave hints, but nothing clear enough to form a complete idea.

Louisa leaned in closer, her eyes narrowing as she tapped a small drawing on the page. "This one here," she whispered, pointing at a swirling wave symbol. "Doesn't it remind you of the old beams down at the pier?"

Gigi's heart skipped a beat. "The pier..." she murmured, suddenly remembering a faint carving she'd seen there as a child, back when she and Willi would play on the docks after school. She'd thought it was just a weathered mark left by some sailor, nothing worth thinking about. But seeing it here, drawn with such deliberate care, she realized there might have been more to it.

"It could be a secret language, or a code, or a map," Louisa said slowly, feeling a surge of excitement as the pieces started to connect.

Gigi's head snapped up at the word "map."

"A map?" Louisa said again. She looked back at the symbols. "Willie might have been mapping out these symbols around town—recording the locations of important sites. But why?"

Gigi's brow furrowed as she studied the page. Louisa sighed.

"I don't know, Gigi. It might be a dead end. But if these are clues he left, then it's like he was trying to lead someone... maybe us... to something."

Gigi nodded, her fingers tracing the wave symbol before moving to another—a crescent moon she recognized from one of the journal's earliest pages.

"The crescent?" Louisa looked closer. "I think I've seen it before, too. Somewhere near the general store."

The realization made Gigi's breath catch. What if the symbols scattered around Haven's Reach were more than random carvings? What if they were a hidden code, pointing to secrets her brother had been chasing? Her fingers tingled as she turned the page, feeling as if she were uncovering Willie's journey one layer at a time. She turned to Louisa, a spark in her eye.

"You want to find them," Louisa said, her own excitement growing. Gigi nodded. "Well, I'm in. If Willie left these as clues, then we're going to follow them."

An hour later, Gigi and Louisa were making their way down the cobblestone path toward the pier, the evening fog settling thickly around them. The faint smell of saltwater filled the air, mixing with the earthy scent of wet stone and moss. The pier stretched out ahead, its beams creaking with age, and Gigi felt a strange mixture of excitement and nervousness settle in her stomach.

She led Louisa toward the old dock, where the wood was worn and smooth from years of salt air and ocean spray. The faint sound of waves slapping against the posts was almost rhythmic, setting a slow, deliberate beat as they scanned the beams.

Gigi stopped, pointing to a faint, swirling shape carved into the post closest to the water.

Louisa crouched down, brushing her fingers over the marking. "It's the same as in the journal. This must be one of the symbols Willie saw." She glanced up at Gigi, a mix of excitement and fear in her eyes. "What do you think it means? A signal? Maybe to let people know where to meet?

Gigi shook her head, kneeling beside her friend. It could be a meeting place... or it could be a warning.

The carving was barely visible in the dim light, but Gigi could make out the lines of the swirling wave. She couldn't help but wonder if her brother had crouched here, too, tracing the same lines, trying to uncover the same mysteries she was.

As they moved further down the dock, they found a second symbol—a small, faint crescent moon carved into the edge of a post closer to the shore. Gigi's heart raced as she recognized it from the journal, another piece of Willie's hidden map revealing itself. She reached out to touch it, feeling a strange connection to her brother, as if his hands had been here too, reaching out through time to guide her.

'This has to mean something,' she thought, her internal voice almost lost in the sound of the waves. 'Willie must have left these symbols to tell us where he'd been. Maybe he wanted us to follow his path, to find what he was looking for.'

Gigi nodded, a determined look in her eyes. If he thought these were important enough to record, then there's more to this story. She needed to keep going.

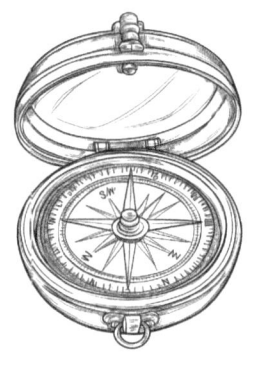

Chapter 12

Chasing Ghosts

The next morning, the girls set out again, following the clues they'd uncovered in Willie's journal. Each symbol seemed to lead them to a new location in town, and each stop brought more questions. Outside the general store, they found another mark—a crescent moon half-hidden in the stone foundation. The sight sent a thrill through Gigi, confirmation that they were on the right track.

"Why would anyone put these symbols here?" Louisa muttered, glancing around as if she expected to see someone watching. "It's like a trail, but I don't understand what it's supposed to lead to."

Gigi felt the same way. Each symbol felt like a breadcrumb leading them through the mystery, yet the meaning behind it all remained elusive. Her brother had clearly been onto something, something important; but what?

They moved on, finding more symbols outside the café and even on a small stone near the post office, each marking like a piece of the town's hidden history. With each discovery, the mystery deepened, pulling them further in.

As they examined the symbol on the stone by the post office, Louisa hesitated, her gaze flickering to Gigi. "Do you think anyone else knows about these? I mean... other than Willie?"

Gigi's stomach twisted, her mind flashing back to the museum and Mr. Thornton's cryptic warnings. He'd spoken of certain townsfolk, hinted that not everyone in Haven's Reach was as innocent as they seemed. And these symbols... they all seemed to lead back to places the museum had either sponsored or displayed.

Gigi nodded slowly, her eyes narrowing. "Mr. Thornton."

Louisa's eyes widened, her voice dropping to a whisper. "You think Mr. Thornton might be involved?" She leaned in closer. "I guess he might know something. I mean, he knew Willie, and he encouraged you to keep asking questions. But these marks everywhere... you think he knew about them all along?"

Gigi pondered the question for a moment. The symbols led back to places connected to the museum. What if he'd been using the museum to cover up whatever these markings meant?

Gigi exchanged a tense look with Louisa, the weight of their discovery settling over them. Mr. Thornton had always seemed trustworthy, a man deeply invested in Haven's Reach and its history. But now, with each symbol they uncovered, the possibility grew more real. If he knew about Willie's investigation... he could be connected to the mystery in ways Gigi hadn't imagined.

"Gigi," Louisa said, her voice thick with worry, "if Mr. Thornton is part of this, then we have to be careful. He knows a lot about the town, about its secrets."

Gigi nodded, her gaze hardening with resolve. They needed to go to the museum tonight. She didn't think he'd tell them everything outright. They needed to see for themselves if there were more symbols... or if he was hiding anything else.

A thrill of fear mixed with excitement raced through her. With each new clue, each hidden marking, she felt closer to finding the truth about her brother, even if it meant confronting Mr. Thornton and whatever secrets the museum held.

The night air was cool and thick with fog as Gigi and Louisa made their way toward Haven's Reach Historical Museum. The streetlamps cast eerie pools of light onto the cobblestone street, their glow barely piercing the mist that curled around the town like ghostly fingers. The girls walked quickly, their footsteps muffled against the stone, each of them glancing over their shoulders as if expecting to see Mr. Thornton lurking in the shadows.

The museum loomed ahead, its stone walls damp with mist, the faint glow of lights from within casting distorted shapes through the old, wavy glass windows. The thought of returning here after hours filled Gigi with a mixture of excitement and trepidation. She had spent many afternoons in the museum, marveling at its collections, listening to Mr. Thornton's stories. But tonight, with the knowledge they'd uncovered, the place seemed different—less a beacon of history and more a vault of secrets.

Gigi felt Louisa's hand on her arm, grounding her. "Are you sure about this, Gigi? Mr. Thornton... he's always been so kind. But if he's involved..."

Gigi's jaw tightened as she glanced at her friend. It was hard to believe, but every clue they'd found—the symbols, the map, the connection to Willie—seemed to lead back here, or to places connected with the museum. And Mr. Thornton hinted that certain people in town couldn't be trusted. Perhaps he meant himself, also.

The thought sent a chill down Gigi's spine. She had trusted Mr. Thornton, looked up to him as a wise mentor who cherished history and knowledge. But now, with each new clue, she felt the trust slipping away, replaced by a growing suspicion. She took a steadying breath, determined to uncover the truth, even if it meant confronting the museum's secrets. They'd begin at the entrance; perhaps there were more symbols around the door.

The girls crept forward, their eyes scanning the stone archway that framed the museum's entrance. Gigi's heart pounded as she traced her fingers along the cool, damp stone, feeling for any indentations. It didn't take long to find what she was looking for—a faint, star-shaped symbol carved into the stone just beneath a layer of grime and moss.

Gigi's fingers trembled as she brushed away the debris, revealing the symbol in full. It matched one of the final symbols in Willi's journal, one he'd drawn with extra care, as if it held special significance.

"What is that?" Louisa asked. "Is that..." She paused. "It is! It's a sign, Gigi! Maybe a marker showing us that the museum is a central point... or a meeting spot." Louisa's face grew pale in the dim light. "So Mr. Thornton could be using the museum for more than just displaying artifacts. It could be where he meets with the others."

Gigi nodded, a grim determination settling over her. There was only one way to know for sure. They needed to get inside and see if there are any more of these symbols hidden in the exhibits. If there were... then maybe they led to something Mr. Thornton didn't intend for anyone to find.

They circled around to the back, where a small window was cracked open just enough to let in a draft. Gigi boosted Louisa up, her heart pounding as she glanced around to ensure they weren't being watched, and then climbed in herself, landing softly on the wooden floor. The museum was silent, its shadows stretched long and distorted in the faint light filtering in from the street.

Gigi stopped; it felt like she was being watched. Slowly she scanned the room; she and Louisa were the only ones there. A slight movement caught her eye. They were spotted!

A gray cat slipped out from behind a shelf and jumped onto a display case. It sat on its haunches and watched the girls.

"That's a pretty cat," Louisa said. "I wonder what it's doing here?" Gigi shrugged.

They made their way through the main exhibit hall, careful to keep their footsteps light, each sound seemingly amplified in the stillness. Glass cases displayed ancient maps, pottery shards, and faded paintings of Haven's Reach, all remnants of a forgotten time. Gigi felt a pang of nostalgia as she glanced at the familiar displays, memories of simpler days when she'd roamed the museum halls without suspicion.

"Where should we start?" Louisa whispered, her gaze darting around the dim room.

Gigi thought back to the symbols they'd discovered around town, each one marking a significant location tied to Willie's investigation. His notes kept circling back to the sea, the smugglers, and the Golden Anchor. It would make sense that if anything was hidden, it was probably in the maritime exhibits.

Gigi took Louisa's hand and led the way. They moved quickly, their shadows gliding over the polished floors as they made their way to the maritime wing. The familiar scent of old wood and salt lingered in the air, mixing with the faint mustiness of aged artifacts. Rows of glass cases displayed models of old ships, navigational tools, and maps of the coastline from centuries ago.

Louisa stopped beside a display of an old, weather-beaten map that depicted the coastline of Haven's Reach. She gasped softly, pointing to a small, swirling wave symbol inked into a spot near the lighthouse.

"Gigi, look," she whispered, tracing the symbol with her finger. "It's the same wave symbol from the pier. Do you think this map could have been part of the smugglers' operations?"

Gigi's heart raced as she studied the map, her fingers brushing over the glass. It had to be. And if Mr. Thornton knew about this, then he must have known where the smugglers operated. He might have even used this map to keep track of their activities. Gigi gave Louisa a knowing look and nodded once.

They moved on, scanning each display for more symbols. Gigi felt a growing sense of urgency, as if they were racing against an invisible clock. Her eyes landed on a brass compass encased in glass, the faintest carving of a crescent moon etched into its frame. The sight of it made her breath catch—it was nearly identical to the compass she'd found near the wreckage of the Golden Anchor.

"That compass..." Louisa whispered, her voice trembling. "It's like the one you found by the wreck. And it has the same crescent moon symbol we saw by the general store." Her face paled as she studied it. "Mr. Thornton must have known Willie had the other compass. He might have even given it to him. Do you think he's been... guiding Willie through this mystery, the same way he's been guiding us?"

The possibility sent a shiver down Gigi's spine. If Mr. Thornton had given Willie clues, leading him into the same investigation, then he could have been involved from the very beginning. And if Willie's trail led to danger, then Mr. Thornton might have had a hand in it all.

They continued moving through the exhibits, finding symbol after symbol hidden on old artifacts and maps, each one matching a clue in Willi's journal. It was as if the museum itself was a puzzle, each piece leading them deeper into the mystery, but none offering clear answers.

Finally, Gigi stopped in front of a glass case displaying an intricately carved wooden box. The box was dark and weathered, covered in swirling patterns and symbols she didn't recognize. But near the bottom corner, just barely visible, was a star symbol, similar to the one they'd seen outside the museum door.

Louisa's voice trembled as she spoke. "Gigi, I think this box could be connected to the symbols we found. What if it holds something important?"

Gigi's pulse quickened, the thought sparking a wild hope inside her. They had to open it. But as she looked around, searching for some way to access the case, the sound of a soft creak echoed through the museum, cutting through the silence like a knife. Gigi froze, her heart pounding, her gaze darting to the source of the sound.

Mr. Thornton stood at the far end of the room, his expression unreadable in the dim light. His gaze settled on Gigi and Louisa, his mouth set in a hard line.

"So," he said quietly, his voice filling the empty hall, "you two have been very busy, haven't you?"

The words hung in the air, heavy with meaning, and Gigi felt a wave of fear mixed with defiance. She squared her shoulders, refusing to back down.

"We know you're involved, Mr. Thornton," Louisa said, her voice trembling. "You know about the symbols, the smugglers, everything. Why are you hiding it?"

Mr. Thornton let out a long sigh, his face softening for just a moment before it hardened again.

"It's more complicated than you understand, girls. Some secrets are meant to stay buried."

Gigi took a step forward, her gaze unwavering. "Willie."

Mr. Thornton hesitated, his hand clenching and unclenching at his side. "Your brother... he was determined to find answers, just like you. But he didn't understand the risks, the dangers that come with digging too deep. I tried to warn him, but he wouldn't listen. And now you're making the same mistakes."

Gigi's chest tightened as his words sank in.

"You knew something would happen to him," Louisa whispered, her voice barely audible. "And you let it happen?"

Mr. Thornton's gaze flickered with something that looked like regret, but his expression quickly hardened again. He looked from Louisa to Gigi.

"Your brother's choices were his own, Gigi. He was drawn to these secrets, just as you are. But there are things in this town that should remain hidden. The smugglers... the symbols... they're part of a legacy that stretches back centuries. And if you're not careful, you'll find yourself trapped in the same web."

Louisa's voice broke through the silence, trembling with fear. "What kind of legacy are you talking about?"

Mr. Thornton's eyes seemed to darken as he looked at them, his voice dropping to a whisper. "A legacy of power, of secrets buried beneath the waves and whispered through generations. The symbols... they're a map, yes, but they're also a warning. They mark the places where history's shadows still linger. And anyone foolish enough to follow them risks being caught in those shadows."

Gigi's resolve only deepened, her fear overshadowed by her determination to find out the truth about her brother. "Then I'll take that risk," she said, her voice steady. "Because I won't let Willie's story end in the shadows."

Mr. Thornton's gaze softened, a flicker of something almost like sadness in his eyes. "You're a brave girl, Gigi. Braver than most. But bravery can be dangerous when it's misguided. If you continue down this path... just be prepared for what you'll find."

Without another word, he turned and walked away, his footsteps echoing through the empty museum. Gigi and Louisa exchanged a glance, both of them shaken, but their determination stronger than ever.

"We're close, Louisa," Gigi whispered, clutching Willie's journal tightly. 'Closer than we've ever been,' she added in her thoughts.

Louisa nodded, her eyes alight with the same fierce resolve. "Then we'll keep going. No matter what."

Together, they slipped back out into the night, the weight of Mr. Thornton's words settling over them, but their hearts set on the truth.

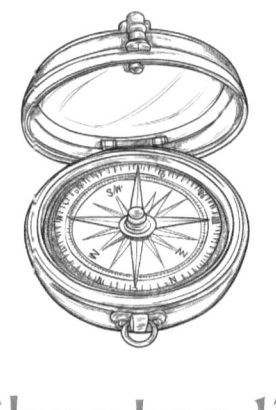

Chapter 13

The Lost Message

Gigi and Louisa stepped out of the museum, their hearts still racing from the confrontation with Mr. Thornton. The night had grown colder, and the fog wrapped tightly around Haven's Reach like a thick, damp blanket. The sharp scent of saltwater hung in the air, and the faint sound of the crashing waves echoed in the distance, blending with the distant creak of old wooden structures that lined the streets.

Gigi shivered, both from the cold and from the lingering tension that still clung to her after their encounter. She pulled her jacket tighter around her, feeling the damp fabric against her skin as she glanced at Louisa, who was staring ahead, her brow furrowed.

"What do you think he meant?" Louisa whispered, her breath misting in the cool air. "About legacies and shadows?"

Gigi's heart thudded heavily in her chest. Mr. Thornton's words had been cryptic, but there was something deeply unsettling about them, something that resonated with the mystery they had been unraveling. She shook her head, her voice barely above a whisper. "I don't know." 'But whatever it is,' she thought, 'it's tied to those symbols—and to Willie.'

They walked in silence for a few moments, the quiet of the town at night adding to the eerie atmosphere. The cobblestones under their feet were slick with moisture, making their footsteps sound soft, almost muffled. The normally bustling town felt empty, as though everyone had retreated behind locked doors, leaving the girls alone in the misty night.

Suddenly, Gigi stopped. Her eyes caught something out of place on the pavement beneath their feet—something that glimmered faintly in the moonlight, just barely visible in the swirling fog. She knelt down, brushing away a layer of wet leaves, revealing another star-shaped symbol carved into the stone.

Louisa crouched beside her, her voice tense. "Another symbol. Right in front of the museum."

Gigi's fingers traced the carving, feeling the dampness of the stone under her fingertips. The symbol was sharp, clean—newer than the others they had found around town. She glanced up at Louisa, her mind racing. 'He's been leaving these symbols for us to find,' she thought. 'Mr. Thornton must have known we'd come this way. He's been guiding us... but where?'

"That one doesn't look very old," Louisa said. "Who do you think carved it?"

Gigi gave her a knowing look, then looked back towards the museum.

"Mr. Thornton?" Louisa's eyes widened, her breath catching. "The museum. It's more than just a meeting place. He wanted us to follow the symbols here for a reason."

Gigi felt a surge of frustration. The pieces were there, scattered before them like fragments of a puzzle, but the image was still unclear, like trying to see through fog. She stood up, brushing her hands on her jacket, the cold seeping deeper into her bones. 'We're missing something,' she thought. 'He knows more than he's letting on.'

Louisa nodded, standing beside her. The night felt heavier now, the fog thicker, the weight of their discovery pressing down on them both. "Maybe we should go back tomorrow," Louisa suggested. "Go inside during the day when he's not watching us."

Gigi shook her head, her determination burning brighter.

"Then when?" Louisa asked. "He'll expect us another night. Unless..." Her eyes widened. "You don't want to go back tonight? Gigi, we can't!" Her voice was growing frantic. "What if he catches us again? He might not let us go this time!'

Gigi looked at her friend and sighed. If they waited, they might lose their chance. Mr. Thornton was hiding something, and she didn't think he'd let them get close again if they didn't act now. However, Louisa was right; it could be very dangerous to go right back to the museum.

They walked in silence again, the quiet stretching between them, punctuated only by the distant sound of waves and the occasional gust of wind that sent a chill through the streets. Gigi's mind was a whirlwind of thoughts—Mr. Thornton's cryptic warnings, the symbols scattered around town, Willie's journal. Each clue seemed to pull them closer to something, something dangerous and dark, but she couldn't stop now. She wouldn't.

Finally, they reached the edge of town, where the fog grew thicker still, obscuring the rocky path that led toward the cliffs. Gigi stopped, looking out toward the dark outline of the Crooked Lighthouse in the distance, its twisted form barely visible through the mist. The lighthouse had been where it all began—the first clue, the first mystery. And now, it seemed to loom over everything, like a beacon calling them back.

But it wasn't the lighthouse Gigi was focused on now. She turned back toward the museum, her eyes narrowing as she studied the building in the distance, its dark silhouette stark against the night sky. The symbols had led them here for a reason. If Mr. Thornton was hiding something inside, they needed to find it.

Louisa hesitated, her face pale in the dim light. She understood the look in her friend's eyes. "Are you sure?" she asked. "What if he's still there?"

Gigi clenched her fists, pushing down the fear that threatened to overwhelm her. After a moment's hesitation she nodded. 'I don't care,' she thought. 'I need to know the truth.'

They turned back toward the museum, the fog swirling around them like a living thing, heavy with secrets and shadows. Gigi's heart pounded as they approached the back of the building once more, slipping through the same window they had used earlier, the silence inside thick and oppressive.

The museum was dark, its exhibits looming like silent sentinels in the gloom. The faint smell of old wood and musty air clung to the room, mingling with the scent of damp stone. Gigi moved carefully, her eyes scanning the shadows for any sign of movement, her ears straining for the slightest sound.

Louisa followed close behind, her breath shallow as they crept through the maritime exhibits again, their footsteps barely making a sound on the polished wood floors. Gigi's pulse quickened as they approached the same glass case where they had seen the intricately carved wooden box—the one with the star symbol etched into its surface.

Gigi pointed, her eyes locked on the box.

Louisa stepped closer, her voice tense. "What do you think it holds?"

Gigi didn't answer. Instead, she reached out, her fingers hovering just above the glass case, feeling the cold air around it. The box was small, but something about it drew her in, like it was calling to her. Without a second thought, she pressed her hand against the glass, searching for a way to lift it.

Louisa looked around nervously, keeping her voice low. "Do you think there's a way to get the case open?"

Gigi studied the case closely, her fingers brushing the edge where the glass met the wooden frame. She gave her friend a look, raising her eyebrow until Louisa got the hint.

Together, they searched the case, their fingers skimming over the wood, but it was solid, sealed tight. Frustration welled up in Gigi, but she forced herself to stay calm, her mind racing for another solution.

"There might be a key," Louisa said, her voice shaking slightly. "Or maybe... maybe Mr. Thornton keeps it somewhere."

Gigi's eyes flicked to the curator's desk at the far end of the room. The wooden drawers were slightly ajar, as though hastily closed. Her heart skipped a beat. If Mr. Thornton had the key, it would be there.

She moved toward the desk, her breath quickening. Each drawer creaked slightly as she pulled it open, revealing papers, small artifacts, and various old tools. But there, nestled in the back of the bottom drawer, was a small, rusted key.

Gigi's hands trembled as she held it up, the metal cool against her skin. 'This has to be it,' she thought, turning back toward Louisa, who was watching with wide eyes.

Without wasting another second, Gigi fit the key into a small, nearly invisible lock on the side of the glass case. It clicked softly, the sound reverberating in the silent room. She lifted the lid slowly, her heart pounding as the glass swung open.

Louisa's breath caught as Gigi reached for the wooden box, its surface smooth and polished, despite the ancient carvings that adorned it. Gigi's fingers brushed over the star symbol etched into the corner, the same symbol they had seen outside the museum. She hesitated for a moment, a strange sense of foreboding settling over her, but then she opened the box.

Inside, resting on a bed of velvet, was a small, leather-bound journal. Gigi's breath hitched as she picked it up, the leather soft and worn, the edges frayed. She flipped it open, her eyes scanning the pages. They were filled with handwritten notes, similar to those in Willie's journal—symbols, maps, names, dates—but these were older, more faded.

Louisa peered over her shoulder, her voice barely above a whisper. "What is it?"

Gigi turned the page, her fingers trembling. The writing was scrawled, almost frantic, but one entry caught her eye, the words etched deep into the page as if written in a moment of panic:

"The symbols lead to the truth. They mark the path to the treasure, but they also mark the danger. The smugglers knew. They left the clues, but they left the curse as well. Those who follow will be lost in the shadows."

Gigi's stomach dropped, a cold wave of fear washing over her. The journal wasn't just a record of the symbols—it was a warning.

"They knew," Gigi whispered, her voice trembling. The smugglers knew that anyone who tried to follow the symbols would be caught in the same trap.

"Knew what?" Louisa asked, then read over Gigi's shoulder. Her face went pale, her fingers gripping Gigi. "What are we going to do?"

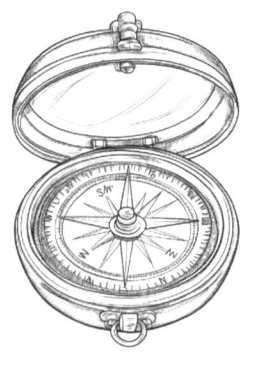

Chapter 14

The Silent Light

Gigi's fingers trembled as she turned the weathered pages of Willi's journal. The leather binding felt warm against her palms, as though it still carried some essence of her brother. Her bedroom lamp cast long shadows across the walls, making the familiar space feel strange and secretive. Outside, the distant sound of waves breaking against the Haven's Reach shoreline provided a melancholy rhythm to her thoughts.

She paused at a dog-eared page covered with Willi's distinctive handwriting. The symbols he'd sketched—waves, anchors, stars—had seemed like mere doodles at first. Now they revealed themselves as something far more deliberate. A map. A code. A warning.

Mr. Thornton's words from their last encounter at the museum echoed in her mind. His voice had dropped to a whisper as he'd leaned close, ostensibly showing her a glass case of native artifacts.

"Curious minds often find themselves in curious predicaments, Miss Ganch. Some secrets are meant to stay buried." His eyes had held hers for a beat too long, his smile never quite reaching them. "Like artifacts in the deep. Better preserved when left undisturbed."

The memory sent a chill through her that had nothing to do with the evening breeze coming through her open window. She'd nodded politely then, but inside, something had shifted. The curator's words weren't just advice—they were a warning.

Gigi studied the journal page again, tracing the symbols with her fingertip. Each mark corresponded to a location in Haven's Reach—the wave symbol appeared near the pier, the crossed lines near the railroad junction, the circle with a dot inside it positioned precisely where the General's Store stood. For weeks, she'd been trying to decipher what they meant, following trails that led nowhere, searching for connections.

Tonight, everything changed. The pattern emerged with sudden clarity, like stars appearing after cloud cover lifts. Every symbol, every mark formed a network across the town map, and all paths led to a single destination marked with a square divided into four parts.

The museum.

Gigi's breath caught. She grabbed her own notebook and quickly sketched the pattern, confirming what she'd discovered. There was no mistaking it. Whatever Willi had been tracking, whatever had ultimately led to the Golden Anchor's mysterious sinking, it centered on Mr. Thornton's museum.

The realization settled like a stone in her stomach. Mr. Thornton wasn't just the curator of Haven's Reach history—he was actively shaping it, concealing parts of it. The timing of exhibitions, the carefully worded placards, the rooms that remained perpetually "under renovation"—all of it pointed to a man with something to hide.

She closed the journal and held it against her chest, taking a deep breath. The smugglers' operation that had claimed Willi's life didn't just involve the harbor or the cliffs. It reached into the very institution meant to preserve the town's history. And Mr. Thornton, with his booming laugh and twinkling eyes, stood at its center.

Gigi slipped off her bed and knelt beside it, reaching underneath to pull out a wooden box. Inside lay her most precious possessions—a photograph of Willi in his sailor's uniform, a ribbon from her mother's homeland, and a small notebook where she recorded her observations. She added Willi's journal to the collection, then took out a fresh sheet of paper.

Her pencil moved quickly across the page as she wrote a message to Louisa. No elaborate code was needed between them—just enough to convey the urgency without revealing too much if it fell into the wrong hands.

"Found the center of the web. Not the harbor—the history house. T is the spider. Meet me at Willow's at dawn. Bring L's notebook."

She folded the paper carefully and tucked it into her coat pocket. Then she changed into darker clothes—a navy skirt and black cardigan that would blend with the night. She pulled on sturdy shoes, knowing the path to Louisa's house would be muddy from the afternoon rain.

Gigi paused at her bedroom door, listening for any movement in the house. Her parents had gone to bed hours ago, exhausted from their shifts at the mill. The floorboards creaked slightly as she made her way down the hallway, each step carefully placed to minimize noise.

At the front door, she hesitated. The night beyond seemed vast and full of unknown dangers. But Willi's face floated in her mind—his easy smile, his amber eyes alight with adventure. He'd never hesitated to chase the truth, even when it led him into peril. She couldn't do less.

The door opened with a faint protest of hinges. Cool night air rushed to meet her, carrying the scent of pine and distant sea salt. Gigi stepped out into the darkness, pulling the door closed behind her with a soft click.

Haven's Reach slumbered around her, windows dark except for the occasional glow of a late-night lamp. The moon hung low and full, casting silver light across the town's sloped rooftops. Gigi kept to the shadows, moving with the quiet determination that had become her hallmark.

Her path took her past the General's Store, its weathered sign creaking slightly in the night breeze. The place where Louisa had planted one of their notes just hours earlier. Had anyone found it yet? Had Mr. Thornton?

The thought quickened her pace. If Thornton suspected they were closing in, if he'd connected Louisa's notes to Willi's disappearance and Gigi's questions...

A sound stopped her—footsteps on the gravel path ahead. Gigi froze, pressing herself against the wall of the nearest building. A figure moved through the darkness, pausing beneath the streetlamp at the corner. The light illuminated a familiar profile.

Mr. Thornton.

He stood motionless, gazing down the street toward the museum. Even from this distance, Gigi could see the tension in his stance, the alertness in his posture. He wasn't taking a casual evening stroll. He was watching, waiting.

Gigi held her breath until her lungs burned. After what felt like an eternity, Thornton moved on, turning down the street that led toward the harbor. She waited until his footsteps faded before peeling herself away from the wall.

Her heart hammered against her ribs as she continued toward Louisa's house, taking a longer route to avoid any chance of crossing Thornton's path again. The encounter confirmed her suspicions—something was happening tonight, something connected to their investigation.

Louisa's cottage sat at the edge of town, a small structure with window boxes full of herbs and a blue door that always stood out against the weathered gray siding. A single light burned in the front room—Louisa was awake.

Gigi approached cautiously, circling around to the back door as they'd arranged for emergencies. Three soft knocks, a pause, then two more. Their signal.

The door opened almost immediately. Louisa stood there, her normally neat hair disheveled, eyes wide with concern.

"Gigi? What's happened?"

Gigi slipped inside, closing the door firmly behind her. She pulled the note from her pocket and handed it to Louisa, watching as her friend's expression shifted from worry to shock.

"The museum?" Louisa whispered. "Are you certain?"

Louisa's eyes widened as she listened, her fingers clutching the blanket draped over her knees as Gigi laid out her plan. "You really think Mr. Thornton is the ringleader?" she whispered, casting a glance toward her bedroom window as if the museum curator might be lurking outside, listening.

Gigi nodded. 'And if he's been hiding smuggling operations through the museum,' she thought, 'he'll be desperate to cover his tracks. We have to make him show his hand.'

Louisa's hands trembled as she reached for her coat, slipping it on with a determined look. "Alright, so what's the plan?"

Gigi took a deep breath, steadying herself. "A trap."

"A trap?" Louisa asked. "How? Where?"

"The museum," Gigi replied.

A puzzled look crossed Louisa's face. "How can we set a trap at the museum?" Realization dawned on her as Gigi smiled. "You're going to steal something?!"

Gigi shook her head quickly. "Pretend."

"Pretend?" Louisa asked. "How do you... OH!" She jumped up. "You're going to make it look like someone's broken in and disturbed the displays! That way, if he's really hiding something, he'll have to react."

Gigi nodded. 'And if we're lucky,' she thought, 'he'll reveal more than he intends.'

Louisa nodded, her lips pressed into a firm line. "And me?"

"Lookout," Gigi replied. "And..." She paused. If this went wrong, she needed people to know where she went and why. They would have to follow...

"Clues," she said at last.

"Clues?" The puzzled look returned to Louisa's face. "Haven't we followed enough clues? Unless... you want me to leave clues? For people to find?"

Gigi nodded.

"But why?" Louisa asked.

"To help," Gigi answered. "To rescue us if..."

Louisa's face paled, but she set her jaw, nodding with fierce determination. "I'll do it, Gigi. I'll make sure people notice."

The two friends shared a look, a silent promise passing between them. They might not know what dangers lay ahead, but they were in this together.

Chapter 15

Beneath the Lighthouse

Louisa wiped her sweaty palms against her skirt as she approached Porter's Café. The morning crowd had thinned, leaving only a few stragglers nursing their cups of coffee. Perfect timing. She slipped through the door, the familiar bell announcing her presence.

"Morning, Lou!" Mrs. Porter called from behind the counter, her flour-dusted hands working a ball of dough. "The usual?"

"Just a quick cup today," Louisa replied, forcing a casual smile. "Running errands."

She chose a table by the window, one recently vacated. The remains of someone's breakfast—crumbs and a half-empty cup—still littered the surface. Louisa pulled a handkerchief from her pocket and pretended to dab at her face while surveying the room. Three loggers huddled in the corner booth. An elderly couple near the door. No one paying her any mind.

Her fingers closed around the small folded paper in her pocket. She'd stayed up half the night composing the message, crossing out words, starting over. The final version was simple: "Watch the museum—secrets hide in plain sight."

Mrs. Porter turned her back to grab a coffee pot. Louisa seized the moment. In one fluid motion, she lifted the sugar dispenser, slid the note beneath it, and replaced it. Her heart hammered against her ribs.

"Here you go, dear." Mrs. Porter appeared with a steaming cup.

Louisa nearly jumped out of her skin. "Thanks."

She took a single sip of coffee, hardly tasting it, then glanced at her wristwatch. "Oh! I'm running late. I'll have to take a rain check on that cup."

She left some coins on the table and hurried out, feeling Mrs. Porter's curious gaze follow her. Outside, Louisa exhaled slowly. One down, two to go.

The General's Store loomed ahead, its weathered sign creaking in the morning breeze. Louisa squared her shoulders and pushed through the door.

"Morning, General," she called to the gruff proprietor who stood arranging cans on a shelf.

He grunted in response, barely looking up. General Cottontail wasn't one for pleasantries, which suited Louisa fine today.

She wandered the narrow aisles, pretending to browse. A stack of freshly delivered newspapers sat near the counter. Louisa approached, making a show of reading the headlines.

"Anything worth knowing today?" she asked, lifting the top paper.

"Same old," the General muttered. "War news. Politics. Nothing changes."

The bell above the door jingled as a customer entered. The General shuffled off to help them. Louisa slipped her second note—"Smugglers in Haven's Reach?"—between the third and fourth papers in the stack. Anyone looking for a newspaper would find it, but it wouldn't be immediately visible to the General.

She selected a paper for herself and paid, careful to maintain her usual demeanor. As she stepped back outside, her hands trembled slightly. The morning sun felt too bright, too exposing. Every face on the street seemed to watch her with suspicion.

"Get a grip," she whispered to herself. "Just one more."

The walk to the pier felt endless. Louisa clutched her newspaper like a shield, occasionally stopping to pretend to read an article. The town looked the same as it always had—the mill smokestacks puffing in the distance, fishermen mending nets, children playing hopscotch—yet everything felt different, dangerous.

She reached the pier where she and Gigi had first spotted the wave symbol. The wooden planks creaked beneath her feet as she walked to the end, gazing out at the water. A few boats bobbed in the harbor. No one seemed to be watching.

Louisa knelt, pretending to tie her shoe. With quick movements, she wedged her final note—"The truth will come to light"—into a crack between the planks, near the post where the symbol had been carved. The paper was visible enough that someone looking closely would notice it, but not so obvious that it would be immediately spotted.

Standing up, Louisa felt exposed, vulnerable. The open water offered little cover. She turned and walked back toward land, fighting the urge to run.

A figure appeared at the base of the pier—a man in a dark coat, watching her approach. Louisa's heart seized. She forced herself to keep walking at a steady pace, though her legs felt wooden.

As she drew closer, the man tipped his hat. "Morning, Miss Johnson."

It was just Mr. Finch. Louisa managed a weak smile. "Morning."

"Bit early for a stroll on the pier, isn't it?"

"Just clearing my head," she replied, gesturing vaguely with her newspaper. "The fresh air helps."

He nodded, seemingly satisfied, and continued on his way. Louisa exhaled slowly, her pulse gradually returning to normal. She was jumping at shadows now, seeing threats where there were none.

Or were there?

As she walked back through town, Louisa couldn't shake the sensation of eyes tracking her movements. She glanced over her shoulder repeatedly, but saw nothing unusual—just the ordinary morning bustle of Haven's Reach.

The sun climbed higher, but a chill had settled in Louisa's bones that had nothing to do with the temperature. By the time she reached her house, her nerves were frayed to breaking point. She slipped inside and locked the door behind her, leaning against it.

What had she and Gigi gotten themselves into? Smugglers, secret symbols, mysterious ships—it all seemed like something from a dime novel, not real life in their sleepy seaside town.

Louisa moved to the window and peered through the curtains at the street outside. Empty. Normal. Yet nothing felt normal anymore.

She thought of Gigi's determined face, her quiet courage. They had made a pact to uncover the truth, whatever it might be. The notes were planted. Now they could only wait and hope their messages would reach the right people—before whoever was behind the smuggling operation discovered what they were doing.

Louisa sank into a chair, her limbs suddenly heavy with exhaustion. The shadows lengthened outside as the afternoon wore on. She remained by the window, watching, waiting, jumping at every sound.

Haven's Reach had secrets. And now, for better or worse, she and Gigi had declared their intention to expose them.

That night, Gigi made her way to the museum, her pulse pounding in her ears as she slipped around the back. The fog was thick and heavy, rolling in from the ocean and wrapping around her like a damp shroud. The salty air stung her skin, mingling with the faint, earthy scent of the museum's stone walls. She moved with careful, practiced steps, every creak of the floorboards and rustle of leaves sending her nerves flaring.

The back window she'd used before was unlocked, just as she'd left it. She slipped inside, landing softly on the museum's wooden floor, and felt her way through the darkened halls toward the maritime exhibit. The glass cases and shadowed displays loomed around her, their familiar shapes distorted in the darkness, casting strange shadows that seemed to shift with each step she took.

Gigi's plan was simple: she would create the appearance of a break-in, leaving doors ajar and moving certain artifacts to make it look like someone had disturbed the exhibits. If Mr. Thornton truly was the ringleader, he'd be forced to investigate, giving her a chance to confront him and, hopefully, draw out a confession.

Her fingers brushed over the cases as she walked, the cold glass beneath her touch sending a shiver down her spine. She moved quickly, nudging a lantern off its stand, knocking a few maps askew, and leaving one of the display cabinets partially open. Her final touch was a small smear of dirt on the display for the Golden Anchor, a mark that suggested someone had come looking for something.

As she finished her work, she glanced around, her heart pounding with a mixture of anticipation and fear. Everything was in place. Now, all she had to do was wait.

She didn't have to wait long.

Footsteps echoed down the hall, quick and deliberate, and Gigi pressed herself into the shadows, her breath catching as she watched the figure approach. Mr. Thornton's outline emerged from the darkness, his flashlight cutting a swath through the gloom as he surveyed the scene. His jaw was clenched, his expression unreadable as he looked over the disturbed displays, his eyes narrowing.

She was right; he was guilty. If he was only worried about the museum, he would have turned on the lights to see clearly. He would have called the police when he saw the open cabinets. But that would have drawn attention; people would wonder why the lights were on so late. The police would ask questions. No, he had to be guilty. Why else would a curator investigate with a flashlight?

Gigi stepped forward, the silence breaking as she called out, "Mr. Thornton."

He whirled around, his eyes widening briefly before settling into a steely glare. "Gigi. What are you doing here?"

She held up Willie's journal, her hand steady despite the fear prickling her skin.

Mr. Thornton's mouth twitched into a cold smile. "You've been busy, haven't you? Digging where you shouldn't, asking questions better left unanswered." His voice was low, almost mocking, and it sent a chill down Gigi's spine.

"Why?" she demanded, her voice sharp and unwavering. "Willie... You used him."

Mr. Thornton's smile faded, his expression turning hard. "Willie was a liability," he said, his tone as cold as the darkness pressing in around them. "He had too much curiosity for his own good, just like you. The smugglers left their marks for a reason, to keep people like you away. But some of you just don't learn."

Gigi's heart twisted with a mixture of anger and fear, her hands tightening around the journal. "You're the ringleader, aren't you? You've been using the museum to cover up the smuggling, to keep people looking at the past while you profit off the present."

Mr. Thornton chuckled darkly, his gaze fixed on her with a chilling intensity. "Oh, you're clever, Gigi. But cleverness is a dangerous thing. You should have heeded my warning." His voice dropped to a low murmur. "Some secrets are meant to stay buried."

Before she could react, he moved closer, his presence looming, blocking her path. Gigi's pulse raced, but she held her ground, her eyes locked onto his, refusing to back down.

"Where is Willie?" she asked, her voice fierce despite the fear churning inside her. 'You owe me that much,' she thought.

Mr. Thornton's gaze flickered with something dark, a flash of anger and something else—perhaps regret. But his voice was cold and unfeeling. "Willie went tco far, Gigi. Just like you. But if you're so determined to follow his trail, maybe you'll find out for yourself."

He stepped back, his eyes narrowing as he gestured toward the darkness beyond. "The museum isn't the only place with secrets in this town. If you want answers, you'll have to go deeper. But remember—some trails are best left unfollowed."

With that, he turned and disappeared into the shadows, leaving Gigi alone, her heart pounding with fear and resolve. She'd follow Willie's trail, no matter where it led.

Chapter 16

The Final Clue

As soon as Mr. Thornton vanished into the night, Gigi felt a surge of determination swell within her. He'd practically dared her to keep following the trail—a challenge that only fueled her desire to uncover the truth. Her pulse quickened as she slipped out of the museum, the mist curling around her as she retraced his steps. Every sound seemed amplified in the stillness, each shadow stretching and twisting in the fog, but she pressed on, focused solely on the path ahead.

She caught sight of him just ahead, moving swiftly through the fog-draped streets of Haven's Reach, his silhouette barely visible as he made his way down a narrow, rocky path that veered away from town. Gigi kept her distance, ducking behind trees and boulders whenever he slowed or turned, her heart racing as she realized where they were headed—the cliffs.

The salty air grew stronger, each breath thick with the scent of the ocean. The roar of waves crashing against rocks became louder, filling the silent night with a rhythmic, ominous pulse. Gigi had spent many nights near these cliffs, but tonight the path felt different, charged with a dark energy that sent a chill down her spine. She gripped Willie's journal tightly, finding comfort in its familiar weight as she pushed forward, following Mr. Thornton's dark figure through the fog.

The cliffs loomed just ahead, a jagged line against the misty horizon. Gigi slowed as Mr. Thornton reached the edge, pausing to glance around before stepping into a hidden crevice. She watched as he slipped into the shadows, disappearing down a narrow, rocky path that descended into the heart of the cliffs themselves.

Gigi's pulse raced as she crept toward the crevice, peering down into the darkness below. Her instincts screamed at her to turn back, but Willie's face filled her mind, his voice echoing in her memory—a promise that he would always come back to her. She took a deep breath, steadied herself, and stepped onto the rocky path, carefully navigating the steep descent into the cliffside.

The air grew colder as Gigi descended, the dampness seeping into her clothes and chilling her to the bone. The narrow passage was lit only by faint shafts of moonlight filtering through cracks in the rock, casting eerie shadows that danced along the walls. She could hear the distant echo of water dripping somewhere below, mixing with the relentless crash of the waves outside.

Gigi's steps slowed as she reached the bottom, her gaze adjusting to the dim light. She crept forward, careful to stay in the shadows, her gaze scanning the dimly lit cave for any sign of Mr. Thornton or, she hoped, her brother.

The soft scrape of footsteps echoed from deeper within the cave, and Gigi froze, pressing herself against the cold stone wall. Mr. Thornton's voice drifted toward her, low and tense, as if he were giving orders. "Keep everything quiet until the shipment arrives. We can't afford any more risks."

Gigi's chest tightened, her fingers clutching Willie's journal as she strained to listen. Another voice responded, muffled but sharp, and she caught only fragments—something about "the girl" and "keeping an eye on her." She held her breath, terrified they might realize she was nearby, but Mr. Thornton's voice continued without pause, the conversation fading as he and the others moved deeper into the cave.

Once the sounds had faded, Gigi let out a shaky breath, her heart racing as she moved carefully through the cavern. Her gaze drifted over some crates stacked against the wall, each one marked with strange symbols she recognized from Willie's journal—crescents, stars, and waves, all painted in faded ink. The smugglers had been using these symbols for years, marking their shipments and meeting points with the same secret language Willie had been investigating.

Her hands brushed against a small, tattered shoe lying near one of the crates, its faded laces and scuffed leather strikingly familiar. She felt a jolt of recognition—this was

Charlie's shoe. The image of the young boy's innocent face filled her mind, and she felt a surge of anger. He was down here somewhere, caught in the middle of this dark, hidden world.

She moved further into the cave, her breath catching when she spotted a small alcove carved into the rock, dimly lit by a flickering lantern. And there, huddled on the cold, stone floor, were Charlie and Willie.

Her heart leapt as she rushed toward them, her footsteps echoing softly in the cavernous space. Charlie's eyes widened as he looked up, his face lighting up with relief. "Gigi!"

Willie, though weaker, managed a faint smile, his eyes brimming with gratitude and something else—an unspoken warning. He reached out, his hand trembling as she took it in her own, feeling the cold, familiar grip she'd longed for.

"Gigi," Willie whispered, his voice hoarse but full of warmth. "You found us."

She nodded, blinking back tears as she held his hand tightly. 'I promised I'd bring you home,' she thought. 'Both of you.' She looked over at Charlie, whose small face was streaked with dirt but filled with hope.

For a brief moment, Gigi felt a flicker of peace—a fleeting sense that everything would be okay, that she had found her brother, and soon they'd be safe. But that hope was shattered by the sudden scrape of footsteps behind her.

Rough hands seized her shoulders, yanking her back from Willie and Charlie. Gigi struggled, her heart hammering as she looked up to see a group of men surrounding them, their faces hidden in shadow. She recognized the steely glint in their eyes, the cold, ruthless expressions that confirmed they were the smugglers, the very ones who had kept her brother and Charlie hidden in this dark, miserable place.

And there, standing at the edge of the group, his face twisted into a mocking smile, was Mr. Thornton.

"Well, well," he said softly, his voice dripping with satisfaction. "The clever girl finally found her way into the shadows." He looked down at her with a chilling calmness, his eyes gleaming in the dim light. "You've gone too far, Gigi. There are some truths that should never be uncovered."

Gigi's heart raced, but she held her ground, lifting her chin defiantly. "People know," she said at last. "They'll come looking for us."

Mr. Thornton's smile widened, a glint of amusement in his eyes. "Oh, I'm counting on that. But by the time they come, you'll be far from Haven's Reach—just another story swallowed by the sea."

A shiver ran down her spine as the words sank in, the weight of the situation pressing down on her. She glanced at Willie, whose face was pale but calm, and Charlie, who clung to her side, his small hands trembling.

But even in the midst of her fear, Gigi felt a spark of hope. Louisa's notes, scattered around town, had planted the seeds of suspicion. Someone would come looking for them; someone would follow the trail they'd left. And until then, she would fight with everything she had to keep her brother and Charlie safe.

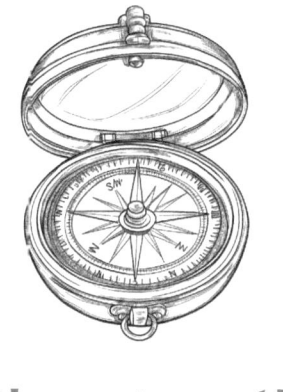

Chapter 17

The Last Beacon

Gigi met Mr. Thornton's gaze, her voice strong and unwavering. "You don't control us."

His smile faded, replaced by a steely glare. "We'll see about that." He nodded to the men surrounding her, his tone cold and final. "Take them deeper into the cave. I'll deal with them myself once the shipment is secured."

The smugglers moved forward, their hands gripping Gigi, Willie, and Charlie as they were forced into the depths of the cave. But even as the shadows closed in, Gigi held onto that spark of hope, clinging to the belief that, somehow, they would find their way back to the light.

As they went deeper the air grew colder, heavier, thick with the metallic tang of damp stone and a foul, briny scent that stuck to their skin. Flickering torchlight cast long shadows on the walls, creating twisted shapes that seemed to writhe in the periphery, as if the very cave itself were alive and watching their descent.

Gigi's heart pounded, the fear swirling in her chest like a storm, but she clenched her jaw, willing herself to stay calm. Willie stumbled beside her, his face pale and thin, but he held his head high, meeting her gaze with quiet determination. And then there was Charlie, small and scared, clinging to Gigi's hand with a grip that belied his young age. She squeezed his hand back, the unspoken promise hanging between them: We're getting out of this. Together.

Mr. Thornton led the way, his figure a dark silhouette at the head of their group, moving with an eerie calm that made Gigi's skin crawl. She'd once trusted him, seen him as a quiet guardian of the town's history. But now, with his true nature laid bare, he seemed monstrous—a keeper not of history, but of secrets and shadows, his knowledge a weapon to wield rather than a gift to share.

As they reached the deepest part of the cave, the walls began to widen, opening into a vast, underground chamber. The ceiling soared above them, lost in shadow, while stalactites dripped water onto the stone floor below, each droplet echoing in the cavernous space. In the center of the chamber, piles of crates, sacks, and mysterious bundles lay stacked, each one marked with the familiar symbols from Willie's journal—the crescent moons, the stars, the waves. This was the heart of the smuggling operation, hidden far from the prying eyes of Haven's Reach.

"Welcome to the vault," Mr. Thornton said, his voice echoing through the chamber with a dark satisfaction. "Not many people get to see this place—and none of them ever leave to talk about it."

Gigi swallowed hard, her mouth dry. She glanced at Willie, who was standing straighter now, his gaze locked on Mr. Thornton with a fierce intensity. Her brother might have been weak, but his spirit was unbroken.

"Why?" Gigi demanded, her voice trembling but steady. "You were respected, trusted. The museum, your knowledge—you had everything."

Mr. Thornton turned to her, his face cast in half-shadow by the flickering torchlight. "Because respect isn't enough, Gigi. People respect what they see on the surface, but power—the kind of power that controls the flow of secrets, of goods, of people—that's what keeps a man truly safe. That's what builds a legacy." He paused, giving Gigi a contemptuous look. "You see, Gigi, history is a commodity, something to be traded, bartered, held by those with the power to wield it. I simply found a way to turn that legacy into something profitable."

Gigi felt a wave of anger boil within her, but she held herself back, forcing herself to listen. "Profitable?"

Mr. Thornton's gaze darkened, his voice low and menacing. "The Prohibition era may have introduced us to a steady stream of income—smuggling liquor to loggers who didn't want the law meddling in their affairs. But when that dried up, I saw an opportunity far more valuable." He paused, his eyes glinting with greed. "Artifacts, Gigi. Ancient native artifacts, each one worth a small fortune to the right collector."

Gigi's stomach twisted as she took in the implications of his words. The artifacts—the relics of the land, of the people who had lived here long before the town of Haven's Reach had been settled. Mr. Thornton wasn't just trafficking goods; he was stripping away pieces of history, selling off sacred items to the highest bidder.

"Those artifacts belong here," Gigi said, her voice trembling with outrage. "They're part of this place, part of its story. You can't just... sell them off like that."

Mr. Thornton's gaze hardened, his expression turning cold and unyielding. "This town's story is one of survival, Gigi. And survival often requires sacrifice. Those artifacts may mean something to the indigenous people, yes, but to everyone else, they're simply relics. Objects to be admired or coveted, to hold or to trade. I found buyers willing to pay for that privilege—and a steady supply willing to help me acquire it."

Gigi's mind spun, piecing together the fragments of the story. Willie's journal, the strange symbols, the carvings near the caves—each one pointed to this operation, hidden in plain sight, fueled by Mr. Thornton's greed. She swallowed, her voice steady despite the anger seething within her. "And you kept Willie alive because you needed him. He knew the caves better than anyone, and he could guide your smugglers through without getting lost."

Mr. Thornton nodded, a small, smug smile creeping onto his face. "Exactly. Willie and Charlie had an unfortunate talent for stumbling upon things better left alone. But as long as Willie could be... persuaded to help, I found it beneficial to keep him around. And as for Charlie," he said, casting a cold glance at the boy, "well, he simply became collateral."

Charlie let out a small, choked sob, pressing himself closer to Gigi's side. She placed a protective hand on his shoulder, her heart aching at the fear in his eyes, but she held her ground, glaring at Mr. Thornton.

"You forced Willie to help," she said at last. "Or else..." She didn't finish.

"Yes," Mr. Thornton said, as if discussing a simple business transaction. "A boy like Willie, with his intelligence, his knowledge of the caves, was a useful tool. But curiosity," he added, his eyes narrowing, "is a dangerous thing. And your brother's curiosity has gotten him in deeper than he realized. Just like yours."

Gigi felt a surge of fury rise within her, the injustice of it pressing against her chest like a stone. Mr. Thornton had taken advantage of everything she and Willie loved about Haven's Reach—the stories, the history, the sense of belonging—to fuel his greed, to satisfy his selfish thirst for power. And now he was threatening to bury it all, along with the people she cared about.

Gigi clenched her fists, her nails digging into her palms. The anger burning inside her drowned out her fear, giving her the strength to keep her voice steady. "People will find out. The authorities, the townsfolk—they're already suspicious."

Mr. Thornton smirked, shaking his head. "Perhaps. But by the time anyone arrives, I'll be long gone. And you three... you'll be nothing more than a mystery swallowed by the tides."

He nodded to the men holding them, a silent command. The smugglers tightened their grips, forcing Gigi, Willie, and Charlie toward the edge of the chamber where a narrow, dark tunnel led deeper still into the earth.

Gigi's heart raced as they approached the tunnel, its depths stretching out like the open maw of some creature waiting to devour them. She could hear the faint roar of water echoing from within, the unmistakable sound of the sea crashing against hidden rocks.

"No," she whispered, struggling against the smuggler holding her. She turned to Willie, her eyes wide with desperation. 'We have to get out of here,' she silently pleaded. 'There has to be a way.'

Willie nodded, his face pale but resolute. "Follow my lead," he whispered, his voice barely audible. "When I make a move, you get Charlie out."

Gigi gave a small nod, her pulse pounding as she braced herself, every muscle tense as she prepared to spring into action. She could feel Charlie trembling beside her, his small hand gripping hers like a lifeline, and she squeezed back, silently promising him safety.

Suddenly, with a strength Gigi didn't know he still possessed, Willie wrenched free of the smuggler's grip, slamming his shoulder into the man and knocking him off balance. The smuggler stumbled back, momentarily dazed, and Willie spun around, grabbing one of the nearby lanterns and smashing it against the stone floor.

The flame caught instantly, licking at the oil that pooled across the stone, casting a blaze of light and sending shadows dancing wildly across the cavern. The smugglers yelled, their attention momentarily distracted by the spreading fire.

"Now!" Willie shouted, his voice hoarse but commanding.

Gigi didn't hesitate. She pulled Charlie close, ducking under the smuggler's grasp, and dashed toward the narrow path that led back toward the main chamber. Her heart thundered as she ran, each step pounding against the stone, the heat of the fire growing behind them. She glanced back just once, her stomach twisting as she saw Willie fighting, his form silhouetted against the growing flames, his determination fierce.

"Come on, Gigi!" Charlie's voice brought her back, his small hand pulling her forward.

They raced through the winding cave tunnels, the air thick with smoke and the acrid scent of burning oil. Each twist and turn brought them closer to freedom, the distant sound of crashing waves their only guide.

But just as they neared the final bend, a figure stepped out from the shadows, blocking their path — Mr. Thornton, his face contorted with fury, his eyes gleaming with a deadly intent.

"You think you can escape?" he snarled, his voice low and venomous. "You're just as foolish as your brother."

Gigi's heart pounded, her hand gripping Charlie's tightly as she stepped forward, her gaze locked onto Mr. Thornton's. "We're not afraid of you," she said, her voice steady, surprising even herself with its strength.

Mr. Thornton sneered, his hand reaching into his coat. But before he could move, a loud crack echoed through the cave, and a boulder dislodged from the ceiling, crashing down between them with a thunderous roar. Dust and debris filled the air, creating a thick barrier that separated them from the enraged man.

"Go!" Gigi shouted, pulling Charlie forward as they sprinted the final stretch, their footsteps echoing against the stone as they burst out of the cave and into the open air.

The night was cold and clear, the stars glinting above them like distant beacons. The salty breeze stung Gigi's face, but she welcomed it, each breath filling her lungs with a freedom she'd thought she'd lost.

And as she held Charlie close, the night air cool against her skin, she whispered a silent promise: she would return for Willie. She would bring him home, no matter the cost. The fight wasn't over—not yet.

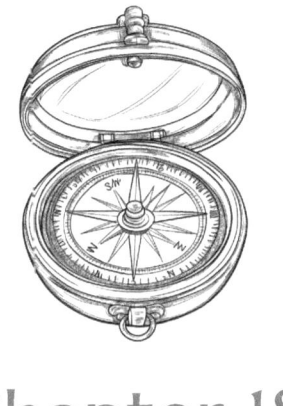

Chapter 18

Crossing the Line

The damp night air clung to Gigi's skin as she tried to catch her breath, her heart pounding against her ribs as she guided Charlie down the jagged cliffs, the roar of the waves at their heels. But the wind carried other sounds: shouting, cursing, and footsteps. Before she knew it, a hand grabbed her arm.

"Run," Willie whispered fiercely. "To the beach. Don't stop."

The moon hung low over the ocean as they raced down the cliffside, their feet slipping on the damp rocks, the waves roaring louder with every step. Gigi's lungs burned, her legs trembling with exertion, but she pushed herself forward, leading them down toward the water, toward freedom. The sounds of the smugglers behind them faded, but the pounding of her heart kept her moving, refusing to slow.

As they reached the beach, Gigi stumbled to a halt, her breath hitching in surprise. Lights bobbed in the distance, growing closer with each second. Figures—men and women holding lanterns—moved along the shore, voices calling out.

Louisa's voice rang clear above the noise. "Over here! Gigi, Willie, Charlie!"

Relief crashed over Gigi like a wave, filling her with a new surge of energy. The authorities, flanked by townsfolk, surged toward them, lanterns casting warm light across the sand. Her grip on Charlie tightened as the three of them stumbled forward, nearly collapsing into Louisa's waiting arms.

"You did it, Louisa," Gigi gasped, her voice hoarse. "You got them here in time."

Louisa's eyes filled with tears, her arms wrapping around Gigi and the boys. "I'd never let him get away with this, Gigi. Not after everything he did."

Behind them, the sounds of the smugglers' frantic shouts grew louder, and Gigi turned, her eyes narrowing as she spotted Mr. Thornton stumbling down the rocky path, his face twisted with fury.

The sheriff stepped forward, his hand resting on the grip of his revolver as he eyed the approaching smugglers. He gestured to his deputies, who moved into position, blocking the only escape route from the beach. "Round them up," the sheriff ordered, his voice low but unyielding. His gaze lingered on Mr. Thornton.

The deputies advanced, and one pointed directly at Mr. Thornton. "You first," the deputy said, his voice cutting through the night air.

Mr. Thornton's sneer faltered as he took in the scene, his jaw tightening as he realized he had no way out. He glanced around the beach, his gaze lingering on each of the townsfolk who watched in stunned silence, shock and anger etched across their faces. The crates of artifacts lay scattered in the sand, illuminated by the lantern light, a damning display of the secret he'd tried so hard to keep hidden.

But his gaze finally settled on Gigi, and the hatred in his eyes was a living thing, sharp and dangerous. His lips curled in a sneer, his voice dripping with malice. "You think you've won, don't you, Gigi?" he spat, his voice low but seething. "You have no idea what you've unleashed. Haven's Reach is built on secrets, on things better left untouched. You may have exposed mine, but this town will suffer for it."

The words sent a chill down Gigi's spine, but she refused to let him see her fear. She straightened, meeting his gaze with fierce determination. "Haven's Reach doesn't need you or your secrets, Mr. Thornton. The town will be better off without you."

Mr. Thornton's sneer deepened, his eyes flashing with fury as the deputies seized his arms, shackling his wrists with a sharp clink of metal. He struggled against their grip, his gaze never leaving Gigi, his voice a venomous hiss. "You'll regret this, Gigi. Mark my words. The town isn't as innocent as you think. And you... you'll find that out soon enough."

With a final, furious glare, Mr. Thornton was dragged away, his curses fading into the night air as the authorities moved him down the beach.

A tense silence settled over the crowd, the weight of his threat lingering like a shadow. Gigi felt Louisa's hand on her shoulder, grounding her as she watched Mr. Thornton's figure recede into the darkness. But somewhere, behind the shocked faces of the townsfolk, Gigi caught a glimpse of Mr. Kline standing near the edge of the gathering, his eyes dark and knowing, a faint nod acknowledging the truth he'd suspected all along.

And as Gigi looked out over the moonlit waves, the faint, echoing roar of the ocean filling the silence, she couldn't shake the feeling that Mr. Thornton's final words held a dark truth she had yet to uncover.

The sheriff's office was crowded and noisy, with voices spilling from every corner of the small, cramped space. Outside, a large group of townsfolk lingered, their murmurs blending into a low, constant hum. Word of Mr. Thornton's betrayal had spread through Haven's Reach like wildfire, each person eager for the details of the secret smuggling ring that had existed under their noses for years. But as people buzzed with questions and disbelief, Gigi sat quietly on a wooden bench near the far wall, her heart racing with anticipation, her eyes locked on the hallway that led deeper into the station.

Willie and Charlie were somewhere beyond that hallway, awaiting their final statements and testimonies. Gigi gripped the edge of the bench, her fingers pressing into the smooth wood, her mind replaying every moment of their escape, every terrifying second in that cave. It had felt so unreal, so far removed from the world she'd known—the world of sandy beaches, summer days, and the laughter she and Willie had once shared. But that world had changed, as had both of them.

The door at the end of the hall creaked open, and Gigi's heart leapt as two deputies led Willie into the room, his wrists free but his shoulders slumped. He looked thinner than she remembered, his skin pale and his face marked by dark circles and a tired expression that made him seem older, somehow. But when his gaze fell on her, a faint, warm smile broke across his face, and the sight of it sent a rush of relief and emotion flooding through her.

"Gigi," Willie said softly, his voice raspy but full of warmth. The deputies led him to sit beside her on the bench, and the moment he was close enough, Gigi threw her arms around him, holding him tightly, afraid to let go.

"Willie," she whispered, her voice breaking. "You're here. You're safe."

For a moment, the weight of everything—the fear, the danger, the uncertainty—lifted, and all she could feel was her brother's presence, his warmth, and the knowledge that they were finally together, free from the shadows of the cave. Willie held her back, his grip just as tight, as if he too feared that this reunion might vanish like a dream.

"Gigi," Willi murmured, his voice barely above a whisper. "I knew... I knew you'd come for me. Even when things felt impossible, I never stopped believing that you'd find a way."

Gigi pulled back slightly, searching his face, taking in every detail of the brother she'd missed so desperately. He was thinner, and his eyes held a darkness that hadn't been there before—a shadow that spoke of hardship, of nights spent in fear and uncertainty. But there was strength there too, a quiet resilience that made her heart swell with pride.

"You kept going, even in that awful place," she said, her voice filled with awe. "You're braver than anyone I know, Willie."

A faint smile tugged at his lips, though his gaze drifted to the floor, his voice turning solemn. "I did what I had to do. Thornton and his men... they left me no choice. If I didn't help them navigate the caves, they would have turned on Charlie, or worse." His voice shook, and he took a steadying breath, meeting Gigi's gaze. "I thought... maybe I could find a way out, a way to expose them. But I was in over my head. If you hadn't come when you did..."

Gigi tightened her hold on his hand, her heart heavy. "You did everything you could. No one blames you for that." She glanced over at the sheriff, who watched them with a mixture of sympathy and firmness, as if he knew the next part of the conversation would be difficult.

The sheriff cleared his throat, stepping forward. "Willie," he began, his tone measured but kind. "We understand you acted under coercion, and we have statements that back up your bravery in testifying against Thornton. That bravery will go a long way. However, there are minor charges to answer for, given your involvement in the smuggling activities."

Gigi's chest tightened, her fingers gripping Willie's hand a little harder. She saw the acceptance in Willie's eyes, the quiet resolve as he nodded to the sheriff. It hurt to know he would face consequences, but a part of her was proud too—proud that he was willing to take responsibility, that he was ready to face the shadows and emerge stronger.

Willie looked at her, his expression steady. "I'm ready for whatever comes," he said, his voice calm. "If this is the price for doing what's right, then so be it."

Gigi swallowed hard, emotions swirling in her chest. "You don't deserve this, Willie. None of this was your fault."

He gave her a gentle smile, his eyes soft. "I knew the risks when I started asking questions, Gigi. And even when things got dark... I never regretted it. I never stopped hoping that somehow, you'd come looking. And you did."

They sat there in silence, the weight of his words settling between them. She could see in his face that he was at peace with the road ahead, that he was ready to take each step forward. But that didn't lessen the ache in her heart, the bittersweet knowledge that they would be apart for a while yet.

The sheriff spoke again, his voice softer this time. "Willie's testimony has been crucial in uncovering Mr. Thornton's entire operation. The court will take that into account. He'll face consequences, but given his cooperation, it's likely he'll be back before long."

Willie gave a small nod, glancing at Gigi with a reassuring look. "I'll be back, Gigi. And when I am, we'll make up for all the time we lost."

A knot tightened in her throat, but she managed a smile, her eyes misting with tears she refused to let fall. "I'll be waiting, Willie."

The sheriff moved away, leaving them alone for a final moment. Gigi clung to it, each second precious, her heart heavy yet full of gratitude. They had survived. Willie was here. And whatever lay ahead, they would face it.

Chapter 19

Sand and Sun

When the deputies finally escorted Willie from the room, Gigi watched him go, a quiet strength settling within her. She knew he would return; his promise echoed in her mind, a steady rhythm that matched her heartbeat. She left the sheriff's office to find Louisa waiting outside, a comforting smile on her face, and beyond her, a crowd of townsfolk gathered, their faces filled with a mixture of awe and admiration.

Whispers of her name floated through the crowd, and someone let out a cheer, soon followed by another until the whole crowd erupted into applause. It was surreal, hearing her name on their lips, the word "hero" murmured in awe. People she'd known her entire life now looked at her with newfound respect, their expressions a blend of gratitude and pride. It seemed that, in bringing Mr. Thornton's secrets to light, Gigi had unearthed a strength in herself she hadn't realized existed.

The crowd parted slightly as Mr. Kline stepped forward, his expression solemn but approving. He inclined his head, his voice quiet but sincere. "Thank you, Gigi. For your courage, for honoring the truth. This town needed someone brave enough to stand for it."

Gigi felt a warmth spread through her, a pride that wrapped around her like a soft, comforting blanket. She nodded, words failing her as she met Mr. Kline's gaze. He gave her a nod of respect, his eyes filled with a knowing understanding, as though he'd known all along that the darkness in Haven's Reach would one day be brought to light.

As the crowd began to disperse, Gigi glanced back at the sheriff's office, where Willie had disappeared, a pang of longing and pride welling up within her. Their lives had changed, marked by shadows and secrets, but she knew that no matter what, they would always find their way back to each other.

Louisa took her hand, her voice warm with admiration. "Gigi, you did something incredible. You saved your brother, and you saved this town. Not everyone could have done that."

Gigi gave her friend a small, grateful smile. "I couldn't have done it alone," she said softly, squeezing Louisa's hand. "Thank you, for being with me every step of the way."

They stood together, side by side, watching as the crowd finally dispersed, the whispers of Gigi's courage lingering in the air like a warm echo. And as Gigi looked out over Haven's Reach, the waves crashing against the shore, she felt a deep sense of peace. For the first time in a long time, she felt truly at home.

The early morning light filtered through the kitchen window, casting a warm glow over the worn wooden table where Gigi's father sat, his broad hands resting on a cup of coffee. Gigi moved quietly around the kitchen, preparing breakfast as she let her father's presence sink in, still adjusting to the new warmth she felt from him. Just days ago, he'd been distant, wary of her relentless pursuit of answers, but everything had changed since the truth about the smuggling ring had come to light.

When she finally set the plates on the table, her father looked up, his eyes reflecting a softness she hadn't seen before. He gestured for her to sit, and she took her place across from him, feeling a hint of nervousness despite herself. Silence hung between them for a few moments, punctuated only by the clink of silverware and the soft ticking of the clock on the wall.

Her father cleared his throat, his gaze shifting to his hands as he toyed with his coffee cup. "Gigi," he began, his voice lower than usual. "I owe you something of an apology." He paused, glancing up to meet her eyes. "And an apology doesn't even feel like enough. I doubted you, doubted that you... that you had the courage and the strength to do what you've done."

Gigi swallowed, caught off guard by the vulnerability in his voice. Her father had always been steadfast, unyielding. Hearing him admit to fear, to worry, was new—something that struck her deeply.

"I only wanted to protect you," he continued, his tone filled with regret. "I thought, if I kept you from asking questions, from wandering into trouble... then maybe I could keep you safe. But you... you did what you felt was right, and in the end, you were the one who kept this town safe. You kept us all safe."

Gigi's heart swelled, warmth spreading through her as she absorbed his words. "I understand, Papa," she said softly, reaching across the table to place her hand over his. "I know you were worried. And I know I can be... a little relentless." She managed a small, sheepish smile. "Maybe more than a little."

Her father chuckled, a quiet sound that seemed to shake loose the last of the tension between them. "More than a little, yes. You've got your mother's stubbornness." He shook his head, but his eyes shone with a pride that he no longer tried to hide. "But that stubbornness—it's what makes you who you are, Gigi. And that's something I wouldn't change, not for anything."

She felt tears prick her eyes, but she blinked them back, her voice a little shaky as she replied, "I promise I'll try to be more careful from now on. I know I worried you... and I don't want to do that again." She met his gaze, sincerity filling her words, though a small, knowing smile crept into her voice. "But I can't promise I won't get involved if something needs solving."

Her father gave a resigned sigh, but his eyes sparkled with understanding. "No, I don't suppose you can. You're too much like your mother, always asking questions, digging up answers. I suppose I'll just have to make peace with the idea of having a sleuth for a daughter."

They shared a quiet smile, a moment that felt like the final stitch mending an old wound. Gigi felt a renewed sense of pride—pride in herself, in her family, and in the strength they had found together. She finished her breakfast with a light heart, feeling that, somehow, everything had fallen into place.

As she left her home in search of her next adventure, Gigi found herself drawn to the beach. There she was at the very shore where the Golden Anchor had first washed up, sparking the mystery that had changed her life. She walked slowly along the sand, the salty breeze tangling her hair and filling her lungs, bringing with it a sense of peace that settled deep within her. The waves rolled gently to shore, their rhythmic sound calming her mind, and for the first time in a long while, she felt a lightness she couldn't quite explain.

She was no longer the girl wandering these shores in search of her brother, filled with questions and fears. She had come full circle, yet everything was different. Her journey had tested her in ways she'd never imagined, showing her the depths of her courage and resilience, and the strength of her bond with Willie. And now, looking out over the vast ocean, she felt at peace with the mystery that had once haunted her.

Lost in thought, she didn't notice Louisa approaching until she heard her friend's familiar laugh, light and teasing. "There you are," Louisa said, grinning as she walked up beside Gigi. "I thought I might find you here."

Gigi smiled, nudging Louisa playfully.

The two friends stood together in comfortable silence, gazing out at the water. After a moment, Louisa let out a wistful sigh, her eyes dancing with mischief. "Remember when we used to talk about finding treasure out here? Or uncovering old secrets about Haven's Reach?"

Gigi laughed, a sound as light as the breeze. "We did more than just talk about it, Louisa. We actually did it. And I think we got more than we bargained for."

Louisa chuckled, nodding in agreement. "So, what's next, Gigi? I mean, you've already solved one of the town's biggest mysteries. Maybe you'll be taking on cases from all over the coast now, becoming our very own girl detective."

Gigi shook her head, laughing. "Don't get ahead of yourself! But... who knows?" She glanced back at the waves, her eyes thoughtful. "Haven's Reach might still have a few secrets left, just waiting to be uncovered. I think I'm ready for whatever comes next."

www.ingramcontent.com/pod-product-compliance
Lightning Source LLC
Chambersburg PA
CBHW052011170626
46808CB00007B/2883